A CHRISTMAS STORY

C J Bernard

HOE BOOKS
2025

This is a work of fiction. Names, characters, places, and incidents are either the product of the author's imagination or are used in a fictitious manner. Any resemblance to actual persons, living or dead, or actual events is purely coincidental.

First published by Hoe Books in 2025
Hoebooks@gmail.com

ISBN 978-1-0682569-9-8

For Freya Bernard & Kathryn Drew

C J Bernard is a lawyer who works in London.

27th November

LARA OPENED HER BLACK cotton bag and took out her brief and the novel she'd picked up at Waterstones on the way to court. After a moment's hesitation, she put the brief back. She had read it yesterday, and again this morning, and it wasn't the most complicated case in the world. The novel looked tempting, and the fact that almost everyone else around her was working added to its attraction. The café, she thought, had the atmosphere of a library. She could hear fingers tapping keyboards and the turning of pages and, in her imagination at least, little sighs of anxiety. The only person talking was a thin man with a thin moustache who was holding an iPhone in one hand and a cup of espresso in the other. Soft winter sunlight caught the edge of his table.

A moment later, Lara looked up and saw walking towards her Jamie Aubrie, father of Poppy and legal owner of the blue cashmere scarf she'd been carrying around in her bag for several weeks.

'Hello Lara.'

'What are you doing here?'

'I have a hearing. Is that OK?'

'I suppose so.'

'Mind if I sit down?'

'As you like. I should be reading my brief.'

'What's it about?'

Lara hesitated. 'A couple, a dispute, let's say it's not all love and roses.'

'What time's your hearing?'

'Eleven.'

'So is mine. Who are you before?'

She told him.

'He can be grumpy,' said Jamie.

'Are you waiting for counsel?'

'No. I'm doing it myself.'

'Good for you. I'm sure you'll be ok,' said Lara.

'Do I hear the sound of counsel patronising a solicitor?'

'No, it's the sound of someone trying to get on with her ex. You always avoided hearings.'

'We change,' he said.

'Yes, we do. Let me know how it goes.'

He grinned. 'I won't need to. You'll be there.'

'What?'

'I saw your name when I signed in.'

'Oh my God, you're on the other side? Why didn't you say so?'

'You didn't ask.'

'Sure it's not against the rules?'

He gave a little laugh and stared at her with his cold blue eyes. 'Because we know each other?'

Know each other? They were together for fifteen years. 'I'm not sure what to say.'

He stood up. 'I am.'

'Go on.'

'You're going to lose,' he said with a smirk as he walked towards the counter in that familiar gangly almost awkward way he had of moving.

So she sipped her only just bearable Ministry of Justice coffee and reached for the brief which had suddenly become a lot more interesting. *You're going to lose.* That was so him. But who was paying for this? Who would have to get on with the other person after the lawyers had gone home? Such a viewpoint, such an either/or viewpoint, such a frankly male viewpoint, made a sensible compromise much more difficult. She'd seen far too often the damage that such an outlook caused. She herself would be sensible. Er, wouldn't she?

'How's Poppy?' he asked as he sat down.

'Hang on, your firm's not on the record.'

'New instructions. Met the client yesterday. How's Poppy?'

'Ok.'

'Ok? Is that all you can say?'

She looked at him in surprise. 'What do you want me to say?'

'I haven't seen her for three weeks,' he said accusingly.

'You cancelled your weekend, Jamie. You said that you were too busy.'

'I had to work and you refused to rearrange,' he said slowly enough to make the words feel like a series of punches. He stared at her for a moment as he had doubtless stared at other opponents in square-ups before hearings but all she could see was how tired and old he looked. There was more grey in his light brown hair and deep lines under his eyes. His usually freckly skin seemed dry and strangely colourless. He hadn't shaved this morning; always a bad sign with him.

'I'm sure that it must be difficult but you're having her this weekend, aren't you?' He nodded cautiously. 'That reminds me,' she added, 'I did say that I'd take her shopping on Saturday morning.'

He gave the impression that he was waiting for that. 'Nothing's changed, has it?' he said, sighing wearily. 'Why can't I take her shopping?'

He'd always hated shopping. 'No, I promised. Girl time, has to be. We'll be back by 12. Is that alright?'

He didn't answer immediately, he just stared out of the window. She followed his gaze and saw the trees, their bare branches touching the snowy clouds. Snow had been falling all day and more was promised.

'It's not right, you know,' said Jamie, turning to look at her, 'that I see Poppy only every other weekend.'

'You also see her every Wednesday afternoon after school. It's what we agreed.'

'Well, I wasn't thinking straight.'

'You had,' she said, remembering the chaos of last year, 'other things on your mind.'

He eyed her carefully. 'In fact, I've been meaning to say, and I might as well say it now,' he paused for a moment, as if he was about to give judgment *ex tempore*, 'that I want Poppy to stay with me for half the week, every week that is. For the next five years, until she's 18. Then she can decide for herself. Of course, she might leave home before then. When it comes to children, you never really know what's going to happen.' He leaned back in his chair with a self-satisfied expression and waited for her to respond. She let him hang for a while before asking if he was joking.

He shook his head. 'Don't you think that it would make things easier for you, Lara?'

'I don't need things to be easier, Jamie. I've a not very nice hangover, otherwise I'm absolutely fine.

'I suppose,' he said, indicating their surroundings with a wave of his hand, 'that now's probably not the time.'

He was backing off already: she would close this one down. 'We don't need a time, everything's ok. She's stable, she's happy. Given what she's been through, we're lucky. She's ok when she's with you?'

But he wasn't listening. 'It's quite common nowadays,' he said, glancing at a woman taking a chair from the table in the corner. 'We could try it for a year.'

That sounded like the compromise offer. 'A year?' she echoed.

She watched him think. 'Even six months.'

When she mentioned the fact that he never left the office until 7.00, he said that 'the partners,' that group of individuals at his firm who had once exercised a significant amount of influence over her life, and perhaps still did, had agreed to his working fewer hours. They approved, he said, of The Plan.

'And what,' she asked, 'do the partners think about school holidays?'

'We'll sort something out.'

'We?'

'I mean, you and me, Lara.'

'And Poppy, she'd have a say, right?'

'Of course.'

'You remember what happened when she stayed that Sunday night with you?'

'Yes.'

'She was an hour late for school, you didn't set your alarm. She'd been up half the night watching films, she didn't have any breakfast.'

'We've discussed that already, Lara. Missing breakfast is not the end of the world.'

She was beginning to get fed up with this bloke. 'Jamie, you're just not interested enough in Poppy. You like the idea of looking after her but that's not enough. Your work and your interests will always come first. You know what the court would say.'

He leaned across the table towards her and for a moment she felt the anger in him. 'I don't care about your fucking court. You have no idea, have you? You've never been apart from her for more than a weekend and you're not willing to imagine what it's like. The thing about you Lara is that you are always, always a lawyer. Facts yes, empathy no. You want to take me on? That's fine, I knew you wouldn't give in without a fight.'

She didn't need this, not before a hearing, not at any time. But when she pushed back her chair, he reached out and gripped her arm so hard it hurt.

'Sorry,' he said, 'I shouldn't have said that. Please stay.'

'Wow. You've assaulted me. That's a first. I wonder what the District Judge will say.'

'You're kidding?'

She made him wait a moment. 'I'm kidding.'

But watching him smile in a way that was so absurdly similar to the way Poppy smiled she found herself smiling too.

'She's ok?' he asked. And somehow he got across the idea that Poppy being ok mattered more than their arguing and more than his apologising and more than her accepting his apology.

'Yes, she's ok, Jamie, I told you, she's ok.'

'How's school?'

'She still loves it.'

'And the journey's not too bad?'

'Half an hour. She goes with Jess.'

'Nice girl,' he said, as he opened his briefcase and took out a shiny Blackwells bag. 'Can you give this to Poppy?'

'Sure. By the way, how's work?'

'Not great.'

For a while, neither of them spoke. Both of them knew that they ought to discuss the hearing but neither wanted to do that. Around them life in the café continued. A balding middle-aged solicitor with a paunch, whom she knew from a particularly fractious service charge dispute the previous year, walked past their table and pretended not to see her. The man with the thin moustache began to gather up his papers. The coffee machine hissed and for a few seconds the ringing of a mobile phone set up a kind of counterpoint until several heads swivelled in disapproval, presumably at the ringing rather than the musical pattern.

Opposite, Jamie was looking at her intently. 'What are you doing at Christmas?'

'I'm trying,' she said, wondering why she hadn't previously noticed his new suit and his lime green tie, 'not to think about Christmas.'

He shook his head slowly. 'You're not really a Christmas person,' he informed her and anyone else who was listening.

'Last year,' she said, 'wasn't great.'

'I hear you drank too much and dropped the turkey in the garden,' he said with a laugh.

'I did not,' she said firmly, 'drop the turkey.' The turkey had in fact slipped off the non-stick tray. At the time, tipping the oil into the flowerbed had seemed the best idea she'd had in ages. But she remembered stepping back on their winter pansies and hearing the bird hit the ground. *Splat.* He was still laughing. She knew she should ignore that. If you want to get on with your ex, you do not argue about whether you dropped a turkey. She knew it wasn't relevant that she had kicked him out a week before the turkey incident. But Jesus, she had to win today.

28th November

WHEN PENTECOST LOOKED UP from his screen and saw Lara Malkova on the other side of the clerks' room, he remembered the call about yesterday's hearing. 'Good morning, Lara,' he said. 'Mr Stewart called. Wanted to talk about yesterday.' One of those solicitors who want you to share their anxiety.

She twisted round and smiled at him. 'I'm sure he does. I'll call him later.' He watched her tap out a message on her phone whilst picking up a brief from her pigeonhole and dropping it in her bag. Of course, he knew that he shouldn't have favourites. Funny, he had thought of her yesterday evening during his Italian class. What was that word? *Sprezzatura*, yes. A way of doing things which makes everything look easy.

'I hear you had Jamie on the other side,' he said, raising his eyebrows without quite knowing what he should be signalling.

Lara stared at him for a moment, seeming to share his uncertainty. 'Yup. It was quite a morning,' she said in the flattest of tones. 'Didn't go well,' she said firmly.

'That wouldn't have been your fault.' They both knew that nine times out of ten counsel make no difference at all, not that you tell the solicitors that. It's all about putting on a show. Most of the time. 'Anyway,' he said, trying to change the subject, 'you'll want me to keep you out of court over Christmas. It will be nice for you to see more of Poppy.'

Her shoulders slumped. 'Actually, after the hearing Jamie told me that he wants to take Poppy to Scotland for Christmas.'

Very occasionally he heard her accent. Usually when she was upset. He'd caught it then. 'He can't do that, can he?'

'He probably can. How's Precious?'

He laughed. 'She's now playing football.' Lara didn't look surprised. He was about to say that if someone had told him thirty years ago that he'd have a granddaughter who played football he would have thought them mad. But then his phone rang. And when he looked up, Lara had gone.

***

Two minutes later Lara opened the door of her basement room and saw Gervase Pooley-Jones sitting behind her desk. He was leaning over a laptop and tapping furiously with two fat fingers. White scarecrow hair, owlish face, glasses with blue frames.

He looked up. 'Lara,' he said, as if he was surprised to see her.

She stood there not knowing what to say. 'Gervase.'

'I meant to send you an email, not just march in like this,' he said. For a such a large man, his voice always seemed to Lara oddly high. 'We had a meeting of the Politburo, I mean the Executive Committee, last night, went on for ages, nightmare, didn't get back until 11. Some of our colleagues, they like talking don't they? I'd been in court all day, a meeting was the last thing I wanted, I can tell you that. I was before Mr Justice Dovey. Do you know him? Brain the size of a planet. I've been before him quite a few times now, he's always nice to me, always gives me what I want.'

'Gervase, this is my room, that's my desk.'

'Actually Lara, that's just it. At the meeting last night we decided to let someone else use this room. You work from home quite a lot, it's only right that you give it up. And the desk, by the way, is not yours, it belongs to chambers.' He leaned back in his chair and peered at the desk showing as he did so a wide expanse of white shirt worn under a grey pinstriped suit.

'It's mine, Jamie's mother gave it to me five years ago. I hired a van and we brought it over.'

'Let's not argue about that Lara, if you want to take it, just let Pentecost know, he can order another. How is Jamie? And your daughter? Potty, isn't it?'

'Poppy.'

'Poppy, yes, that's it. Clapham, you live in Clapham.'

'We live in Clapham, yes.'

'Roderick, I've heard that he lives there, too. Perhaps you're neighbours?'

'Roderick?'

'Sorry, Mr Justice Dovey, he used to be in the same chambers as Jim's former flatmate, or his girlfriend, not sure which. Everyone calls him Roddy apparently, meant to be a really nice chap. Plays squash, that must be really something, to sit as a High Court Judge all day, and play squash in the evening. How exhausting is that?'

'Why didn't the Committee ask for my views?'

'You mean about the room?'

'Yes, I mean about the room. I think it's incredibly bad manners.'

'You've never offered to serve on the Committee, Lara.'

'You meet in the evenings, evenings are difficult. Anyway, what's that got to do with it?'

'It takes up a lot of time, we try and be fair to everyone, that's not easy. But what's wrong with working in the library? Everyone else does.'

'The pupils work in the library, Gervase. Everyone else has a room or shares a room.'

'Lara, I have to get on. I have a skeleton argument to file by lunchtime, my instructing solicitor wants to see it first, though quite what the point of that is, I don't know. I doubt if she'll be able to make head or tail of it, poor love. Extraordinary that we are the beck and call of people who do not know what they are doing, isn't it? Is there any other profession where that happens? Look, I think that you have some junk in here,' he said yanking open the top left hand drawer of the desk.

'It's not junk, Gervase.'

But Lara knew that she didn't have the energy to continue the argument. She went over to the desk and opened her rucksack. 'If you wouldn't mind giving me some room,' she said as Gervase pushed back the chair.

'Be my guest,' he said, with his little laugh.

She crouched down beside him and began to take out the random items which she had put in the drawers over the last five years. It wasn't junk, it was her life. Receipts, birthday cards old and new, letters from solicitors, several briefs, Poppy's school report from last year, letters from the Bar Council, an MOT certificate, several counsel notebooks, an old keyboard, a Miles Davis CD she'd bought for Jamie just before the break-up, draft pleadings, a battered Willa Cather novel, and an unopened packet of Silk Cut. These items were there either because she wanted them near her as she worked or because she couldn't think what else to do with them.

'Does Jamie's firm still instruct chambers?'

'Yes, I think so. Why?'

'No reason. He does property work, doesn't he?'

'Sometimes.'

He might like to see my article in the *Landlord & Tenant*

Review. It was about landlords and cladding. You saw it?'

'I must have missed that one.'

'It came out a couple of years ago. In fact it cites a Court of Appeal case where Roddy - I mean Mr Justice Dovey - was acting. I suppose it wouldn't be *that* odd if I have to refer to it one day, I mean, when I'm before him. Coincidences happen, don't they?'

'I think that they do.'

'How old do you think he is?'

'No idea.'

'You've not been before him? But then I suppose your practice is largely Mags and County Court. Lots of children work, being supportive, showing you care, tea and empathy more than law and facts.'

Lara stood up. 'What do you mean by that?'

'Well, we were talking yesterday about the ambitions we have for chambers, we really want to be one of the best, we want to be up there, Lara, with all the big boys. I can say that, can't I? We shouldn't be doing legal aid work. Everything costs so much. Do you shoot?'

'Not yet,' she said, as she started emptying the drawer on the other side of the desk.

'Snipe, Anna something, shoots snipe, Russia, Tolstoy, isn't it? I've just started shooting, not snipe of course, pheasants. Shame we can't shoot solicitors, that would be fun. Imagine them standing there in their cheap suits begging not to be shot. They'd almost certainly threaten indemnity costs. By the way, do you know how much I pay to shoot?'

'Nope.'

'About £800 a day, and there's all the gear, I ended up buying a dog. That was a mistake, not even sure if he's a pedigree, might be a mix, think I was had. Anyway, best to keep mum about this, we're going to put chamber's rents up, we're going to try and attract a better class of person. There will have to be changes in the clerking. Pentecost, we all like Pentecost, of course we do, but we need someone with a bit more oomph, someone who can market chambers, who can attract solicitors.'

'I get all my work through Pentecost, he's terrific, solicitors love him.'

'There's a girl I know, I mean of course a woman, she's in marketing, works for that Manchester firm which instructs me, she's a bit of a fish out of water up there, it's just a disrepair factory, if we get her on board, the two of you could go out and visit firms. She's very attractive - I can say that, can't I? - you'd make quite a splash. The only marketing we do at the moment is the bloody Summer Party where all the bloody Northern disrepair solicitors come and get drunk at our expense. One of them found his way to *El Vino's* last year and was sick all over the place.'

'I thought that housing disrepair was an important part of your practice?'

'That's going to change, to be honest Lara, it has to, I won't be able to shoot otherwise. A brief fee where the subject matter is a leaking lavatory is never going to be that high. Then there's the cost of training Rupert.'

'Who's Rupert?'

'My fucking spaniel. At the moment as soon as the shooting starts, he runs a mile. I tried to stop him last week and fell over in the mud, mud all over my face, mud on my new jacket, had to get it dry cleaned. That was another twenty five quid. Having a difficult dog is worse than having a difficult pupil. At least a pupil can go out and buy you sandwiches.'

'Poor little dog.'

'Poor little dog nothing. He lives the life of Riley, I can say that, can't I? Anyway, I had better get on, you have everything you need?'

29th November

SITTING AT A TABLE near the back of La Stella waiting for Jamie to arrive, Lara resolved that she would continue talking however annoying she found him. She was far from believing, as some judges seem to believe, that talking is the answer to everything but she knew that the two of them should at least try and reach agreement.

She had suggested to Jamie that they meet after receiving a long and frankly annoying email from him about Poppy and spending half an hour trying to compose a reply which was neither too rude nor too formal. It wasn't easy: she deleted draft after draft. When she finally sent it, he zapped one back immediately, and the speed of his reply was almost as annoying as its content. For a while it seemed as if they were rolling back to a time when angry emails clashed and life was dark and horrible, when it felt that Poppy was the only reason for keeping going. But something made her call him and something made him listen and something perhaps made him speak nicely, for what seemed like ages, telling her what was best for Poppy and what was best for her. He hinted that she wasn't coping and she hinted that he shouldn't be hinting. Here it was, the old problem: how can you have a sensible discussion about yourself with someone who knows you better than you know yourself? But it was true that there had been a couple of occasions over the last few weeks when she had forgotten that Poppy needed a clean shirt and she felt awful about that but as she told Jamie, it was hardly a reason to take Poppy away from her. He answered that he was not taking Poppy away and she knew that wasn't the idea and that she shouldn't overdramatise the situation, dramatising being evidently ok in his book. And on he went. And then on some more. Worlds had been created in less time. When she successfully guessed that he had finished, a small triumph of experience, she suggested a meeting with alcohol to hand. He agreed at once. At least they still had something in common apart from Poppy.

The choice of venue wasn't difficult as La Stella was a favourite place for both of them. She felt that she had eaten off every white tablecloth, sat under every Sophia Loren poster and was more familiar with the restaurant's *decorazioni Natali* than with the ones she had at home. It wasn't the best Italian restaurant in the world, it wasn't even the best Italian restaurant in the Northcote Road. If you sat at the back you had to cope with the noise of the kitchen; if you sat at the front there was the draught from the door. The food was no better than average, sometimes markedly less so. The white wine was never quite cold enough and the red wine never quite warm enough.

She glanced at her watch and saw that Jamie was already five minutes late, which was pretty much par for the course. Behind her, she could hear the beginnings of an argument in the kitchen, whilst in front of her, a bubbling group of young South Africans promised serious noise. Five or six tables had been put together to make one large table which curled around the corner. At Lara's end, a skinny blonde in her 30s was talking to a man called Mike with short brown hair and round glasses.

She texted Jamie a question mark, originally their shorthand for *Where are you, darling?* but which became their shorthand for *Can you let me know where you are?* and then shorthand for *Where are you?* and finally for *Where the hell are you?!!!* But she knew that since their break-up, many of the conventions upon which they had previously relied were no longer in place, and so she followed up the question mark with a *Hope everything is ok, I'm at the back.*

A moment later, he was walking towards her wearing another suit she hadn't seen before. This one was charcoal grey.

'I have a table by the door,' he announced.

She pushed a chair towards him and watched him wince as she caught him on the side of the knee. For a moment he looked at her as if she had hurt him on purpose, but she frowned and gave a little shake of her head and he understood. She saw how sad it was that they each understood each other's tiniest gesture and yet they belonged apart. He nodded towards the other side of the restaurant. 'It's a bit noisy here.'

'It's not too bad.'

He put a hand to his ear, shook his head and retreated, almost bumping into a waiter as he did so. Lara began to read the menu, except that she wasn't really reading the menu. She was pretending to herself that she was reading the menu. In fact she was too busy being cross with their childishness to read the menu, which, in any case, she more or less knew off by heart. But then, without thinking what she was doing, as if her body had taken over, she picked up her glass and began to move in the direction of Jamie's table. And there he was, halfway across the floor, glass in hand. He looked amused. 'I thought you were staying?'

'I'm coming to sit with you.'

'Well, I'm coming to sit with you.'

Oh, God, she said to herself.

Then David, the manager or owner, they'd never really worked out what he was, appeared with a tray. He had a thatch of grey hair, a pointy nose and a slim boyish figure. His flowery shirt was open at the neck. He greeted them warmly but he was evidently puzzled as to what they were doing. 'Everything alright?' he asked hesitantly.

'Yes, thanks,' she answered breezily.

'Yes, thanks,' echoed Jamie.

'You know,' she said, when David had gone, 'this is the first time I've been out for a long time and I'm spending it in the middle of the restaurant floor with everyone looking at me.'

So they sat down at her table and ate the pasta they usually ate and drank the wine they usually drank and talked about the things they usually talked about. They talked of their first flat and of their second house, of people she couldn't remember and of those she'd rather forget. They had conversations which they had never had before and conversations which they'd had on countless occasions. So he told her about growing up in the Scottish countryside with an alcoholic mother and the father he hardly ever saw, and she told him the romantic story of her mother from Sussex meeting her father from Volgograd at a party for journalists in Moscow.

'Where did you live in Moscow?'

'Rublevka. Why?'

'I met a woman last week who'd been to Moscow. I told her about you.'

'You met a woman and you discussed me?'

'Yes, she was interested.'

'Really?'

'I said that you came here when you were 3.'

'I was 2.'

'And that your paternal grandfather was from Moscow.'

'That was my grandmother. My grandfather was from Volgograd.'

'Oh yes, I remember.'

'Have you got a pen on you? '

'Why?'

'So you can take some notes, Jamie. To prepare for your next date. It's nice that I can be of some help.'

'We had to talk about something.'

'You had to talk about something so you talked about me.'

'And it wasn't really a date, Lara.'

'What was it? Therapy?

'Don't be like that.'

'Alright, I suppose you're allowed to go on dates.'

'I'm relieved to hear that.'

'So where did you go?'

'We came here. It's the only place I know.'

They sat in silence until she asked him about his work. For reasons she didn't quite understand, he wanted her to know how tired he was. He was clearly working too hard and not enjoying it at all. His three days in the office would usually end at 8pm and his two days at home no earlier. At weekends, he said, he felt shattered She asked him what he had read recently and the answer was nothing. He had no time during the week and he spent the weekends he had without Poppy sleeping. He asked how his books were, as if he was asking about old friends, and in a way he was. She said that the last time she'd seen them they were just fine. They were still in the attic waiting for a time when he had something larger than a one-bedroom flat in Wandsworth in which to keep them.

'What about your work?' he asked as they sipped their espressos.

'I've been a bit quiet recently, though I don't mind that. It gives me more time to write. I'm planning a series of articles …'

'You don't think that you should move chambers?'

What was it about men and advice? 'I like my chambers, thanks.'

'You haven't thought about going back to where you were before?'

She sighed inwardly and settled back in her seat: he had made up his mind to tell her what to do and so she might as well get it over with. 'You think I should?' As she thought might be the case, his advice was mixed in with reminiscences about the times she'd had in those chambers. He mentioned the clerk who had always liked her, the book-lined rooms and the Chambers Christmas Party where they had met. When he seemed to have finished, she said, 'It's not like changing jobs, you know. I'd have to be sure that my solicitors would come with me.'

But he was no longer paying attention. He had told her what he wanted to tell her and that was all that was important. Now he was sitting up straight and turning his head like a meerkat, his curious way of asking her to listen to the music that was playing. 'You remember how he once played Callas singing Violetta?'

She had almost forgotten the David-once-played-Callas conversation which they had every time they came here. At least she knew what to say. 'Oh yes, wasn't it wonderful?'

'I should ask him to play it again,' he said beaming with pleasure.

But there was something reassuring about having a conversation they'd had so many times before. 'Do you know what this is?' he asked, gesturing towards the discreetly hidden loudspeaker in the corner of the room.

'Gilbert and Sullivan?'

'Very funny. It's Puccini. *La Bohème.*'

'Is that the one with all the coughing?'

He flashed her that Special Look of Disapproval which he reserved for those who do not take opera seriously enough. But the teasing had come naturally to her. It was her defence but it was not a complete defence. What she had found difficult about his love of opera, if love was not too mild a term, was not the time he gave to it, or the money he spent on it, or the music itself, or even the way that she would find under the duvet copies of *Gramophone* and *International Record Review*, and once, a sharp-edged box of CDs of Wagner's *Ring Cycle* conducted by George Solti which Jamie said was incandescent and which she said had scratched her bum. What was difficult was the way in which opera had first call on his emotions. His life with Poppy and herself, she had sometimes felt, was a poor substitute for the rich life he found in opera. The blue eyes of this six-foot former wing forward for Edinburgh University Second XV would glisten as he listened to opera, but he had never cried for her. Not once. But what was his love for her, she used to ask herself, compared to Isolde's love for Tristan? How could life in South-West London measure up to Wagner's supercharged world? How could he mourn Eurydice and then be expected to grieve for Poppy's hamster?

Listening to Puccini now she remembered a Puccini Saturday afternoon one December, when she and Poppy had come home after a day's Christmas shopping to find Jamie lying on the sofa listening to *Madam Butterfly* played at a volume so loud that she had been surprised she hadn't already heard it in Camden Market. He gave her a metronomic nod by way of a greeting, evidently either too tired or too involved with the music to utter words. At the time she had assumed it was the latter. She had sometimes wondered if she should arrange for a screen to be installed at the end of the room. Not for surtitles, he was too serious a buff to require those, but for messages from her and Poppy. *What time does Act II finish? Would you like your supper then?* Or *Your mother called from the hospital. She has broken her ankle. Shall I say that you will call tomorrow or will you need a day to recover?* She remembered how she had turned the music right down, and though she hadn't actually put her hands on her hips, she had given what Jamie later described as 'a little disquisition of displeasure.' She might have mentioned the neighbours, and she might even have mentioned the possibility of the London Borough of Lambeth applying for a Closure Order on the house. When an amused Poppy, who had had to listen to so much loud music from an early age that Lara sometimes wondered whether she would later have hearing problems, had gone upstairs, Lara asked, without thinking, she wasn't even sure that it was she who was speaking, if Jamie might perhaps pay less attention to opera and more attention to her. As soon as she'd asked that question she'd known she had made a big mistake. He'd asked whether she was jealous. Of course she wasn't jealous. Was she sure? Yes, she was sure. You can be jealous, he'd said, without any reason at all. Think of *Otello,* he'd said. We could listen to that together if you like. We could use it to discuss your jealousy ....

Now the music rose to a crescendo and died away. Jamie smiled contentedly with that smile on his face which she had seen so many times before. She felt that if he'd smoked, he'd have wanted to light up. But then he put his elbows on the table and leaned towards her as if he wanted her to see his grey hairs. 'Have you thought any more about what I said?'

She gave him an uncertain smile. 'I've thought of little else.'

That seemed to please him. 'Well?'

'Perhaps I've been too rigid,' she said, noticing now that he had cut himself shaving. 'There seems to me no reason why Poppy shouldn't spend more time with you, long weekends, the occasional weekday night.'

His face fell. The music had already been forgotten. 'I'm not interested in that. If that's all you're offering, then there's not much point in talking.'

Oh, God, she thought, taking a deep breath, he's decided to play the tough guy. 'Jamie, it's all working well. Poppy really enjoys seeing you. She loved going on the London Eye the other week. You're lucky, you know, you have quality time.'

He winced at that. 'I don't want so-called quality time. I think that's a really horrible expression.'

'What are you talking about?'

He took a large gulp of wine. 'I want to see her in her everyday world, like I used to,' he said, gloomily. 'You know, I hardly ever see her when she comes back from school.'

'You don't miss much,' said Lara, thinking of Poppy grumbling about her homework.

He stared at her for a moment as if he was unsure that she was understanding what he had been saying. 'Or when she's looking for her shoes,' he continued, 'or even when she's in a foul mood. When you love someone you want to see them in ordinary time. At the moment, I feel that she's always putting on a show, she's always making an effort.'

'She *does* make an effort – she worries about you.'

He was still staring at her. 'It's almost as if she and I have separated too,' he said. 'It's as if we have to find a new relationship as well … Or do you think that's rubbish?'

It wasn't rubbish at all. She'd advised too many men who had left their partners without realising that they were also leaving their children. It wasn't rubbish, it was the saddest thing in the world. It wasn't a matter of intelligence or at least intelligence as we usually understand it. She put it down to the blindness which anger causes and it doesn't really matter where the anger comes from. They might have been born angry, they might have been bullied at work. Who really knew? They would be shepherded into a meeting room where she would advise them and hope that they wouldn't cry. Occasionally, sitting next to the client would be a new woman, who would be very concerned and comforting and anxious to say that in her experience children are incredibly *resilient* – always, always that word. But Lara couldn't bear to think of Jamie as one of those men and so she moved his sleeve away from the butter and reminded him that it was Poppy's birthday next week.

'I can see her then, can't I?' he asked, almost despairingly.

For the first time in ages, she felt sorry for him. 'Of course you can. Not during the day, we're going to Hampton Court. She's doing a project on Henry VIII, it's called 'Another Difficult Man.' That's a joke, Jamie. Actually, come to think of it, we're going to Amanda's in the evening. What about popping in at around 6?'

'Popping in,' he said, sulkily, 'on her birthday?' He sat back and peered at her. 'You know what's behind it, don't you?'

'Behind what?'

'Your possessiveness,' he said, as if they had discussed the matter a hundred times before. As if, indeed, the fact of Lara's possessiveness had been accepted by the most eminent psychologists on both sides of the Atlantic.

'I'm not possessive, Jamie.'

He lowered his voice to a whisper. 'I used to find it so difficult. Half the time I felt excluded, locked out of my own family.' He sighed. 'But it's not your fault, it's because your mother died when you were young,' he added in a matter-of-fact way as if he was explaining why the car had broken down.

'Jamie ...'

'You want to make sure that Poppy has what you didn't have. Come on, Lara, you used to talk about how you spent your adolescence arguing with your father and missing your mother.'

She couldn't believe this bloke. 'Please don't talk about my mother, Jamie,' she said quietly.

'Alright,' he said, making the cheque-signing mime in a lordly manner to David, who had been watching them from across the other side of the room.

The inference was plain: they would talk about what he wanted to talk about or not at all. They finished their coffee in silence. Jamie looked at his phone and she looked at hers. Around them, the waiters cleared the tables.

30th November

SNOW WAS FALLING AS Lara and Poppy arrived at Amanda's house. It was a red-brick, 1880s terraced house with a slate roof and a green front door which had seen better days. Above the door was a red and green patterned leadlight which had been cracked for as long as Lara could remember. Surrounding the overgrown lawn half-covered with fallen leaves and a thin layer of snow were brambles in which coke cans and takeaway boxes had been caught. One of the cans glistened in the light coming from the Victorian-style street lamp on the pavement outside.

On the way over, trying to keep all emotion out of her voice, she had told Poppy of Jamie's plan.

'So what do you think, darling?' she asked as she held open Amanda's rickety old gate.

'It's cool.'

That wasn't quite the answer Lara had expected. 'Wouldn't you find it difficult?' she asked, anxiously following Poppy along the path.

'Why?'

But Lara's mind went blank. She'd been thinking about this conversation all day, thinking about it while not writing the Advice she was supposed to write, thinking about it while having one-and-a-half glasses of wine at lunchtime, thinking about it as she texted Poppy when she came out of school.

Now all she could think to say was, 'Gym kit.'

'Gym kit?'

'You might leave it in the wrong place or put it in the wrong washing machine,' said Lara.

'I don't leave my books at Dad's,' said Poppy flatly, pressing the doorbell as if to mark the end of the discussion.

Lara tried another tack. 'I think it would be very disturbing,' she said as Poppy stared at her blankly, 'not to have somewhere you can call home. It's wonderful that you go and stay with Dad but this idea is completely different.'

'I'd have two homes, wouldn't I?' said Poppy with that it's-so-obvious tone of voice which Jamie had left behind.

'Not sure if you can have more than one home. Isn't that part of what we mean by home?'

Poppy looked at her as if she was completely mad. 'How long are we going to be?'

Lara waited a moment before answering. Poppy, she'd noticed, was increasingly given to controlling what the two of them talked about. But she did love that confidence. 'Half an hour? You don't mind, do you? I thought you and Jess were friends again?'

Poppy put one finger to her lips and pointed with another to the lighted window on the first floor. 'We are,' she whispered.

'I think that Amanda,' said Lara, obediently lowering her voice, 'wants to talk about moving.'

'You mean,' said Poppy, leaning into the doorbell again, 'you want to talk about what Dad wants.'

Lara decided to ignore that. 'I don't think the doorbell's working.'

'This house,' sighed Poppy, picking up the fox-shaped doorknocker and bringing it down hard enough to make the sound reverberate along the street. In fact, Lara quite liked the house. She'd first come here one hot summer morning fifteen years ago when Amanda and Rob were students at the Chelsea College of Art and the roof was half-open to the sky and there were Rastafarians opposite who could remember having Vivian Westwood as a neighbour. Years passed and Clapham Old Town became fashionable. Bankers replaced the Rastafarians, a couple from Hamburg turned the old corner shop into a deli, and Vivien Westwood moved back.

In the kitchen, Lara told Amanda what Jamie had said. 'He wants everything in place by Christmas,' she concluded. 'And he wants to take her to Glasgow for Christmas and New Year.'

Amanda groaned. 'God, how depressing. You know what New Year in Scotland's like. Lasts until Easter.'

'I'm going to fight it, Amanda.'

'What does Poppy say?' asked Amanda as she slowly made her way to the case of wine by the back door.

Lara hesitated. 'She says she doesn't mind. I don't believe that. She's always been protective of him.'

Amanda bent down to pick out a bottle from the case showing as she did a large split in her jeans. 'How is he? Is he seeing anyone?'

'I don't know, we didn't talk about his personal life. What worries me, Amanda, is that he'd be delayed at the office and Poppy would have to make her own supper.'

Amanda looked at her as if she didn't quite understand the seriousness of the situation, as if she had to concentrate on opening the bottle and finding a couple of glasses.

'That wouldn't be the end of the world,' she said as she poured out the wine.

'I didn't say it would,' said Lara quickly, too quickly really, she had snapped at her. She sometimes wondered what she was turning into.

'Thanks for this. But enough about me. How are you?'

Amanda forced herself to smile as she edged backwards towards the green velvet chaise longue and sat down heavily. 'I'm alright. But Lara, he's still here. I want him here and I don't want him here. How can I want opposite things?'

'Quite easily. I do it all the time. I'm beginning to think that it's the only thing I do really well.'

'Can't you sense that he is here, Lara?' She lifted up her finger. 'Listen. Can't you hear him?'

But Lara could only hear a television on the other side of the wall and the sound of the girls' voices drifting down from upstairs. Amanda had talked about Robert still being in the house before but until now Lara had never understood that she meant it literally. She didn't know what to say. She wasn't really one for ghosts. In matters of the spirit she had probably inherited her father's Soviet outlook. 'I can't hear anything, darling,' she said, sitting down beside her, and putting her hand on Amanda's shoulder.

Amanda bowed her head and sniffed, and sniffed again, and then began to cry. Lara thought that she was used to Amanda crying but she'd never seen her cry as she now cried. What started with little groans broadened out into a great wail which seemed to come from deep inside her. She sat there swaying back and forth as if she was sitting on the edge of a swimming pool and working herself up to take the plunge. Lara held her tight and whispered, 'Please don't cry, please don't cry,' remembering as she spoke all those times over the last year when she'd been the one crying on the chaise longue.

'I can't stand it any longer,' Amanda whispered. For a moment, it seemed as if that statement marked the end of her crying but it started again and this time she began to lose her breath just as Poppy used to do when she was small, and so Lara stroked her back until the juddering stopped and she was breathing more or less regularly.

The kitchen smelt of roll-ups and cannabis, always a bad sign with Amanda. She was wearing her pale blue apron and that grubby old yellow bandana which only came out when she couldn't be bothered to plat or organise or even brush her long brown hair. Robert had died on Christmas Eve almost a year before, but as Poppy had said the previous week, Amanda was still, like, grieving. Photographs of Robert and his crazy metal sculptures stared at Lara from the mantelpiece. Robert in Vienna, Robert in New York, Robert in Woolwich. The room felt like a shrine.

But now the doorbell was ringing. Lara made her way through the damp-smelling hall with the six wellington boots and Robert's black leather jacket hanging on the wonky hook and the framed photographs of sad-eyed dogs from Amanda's childhood. Next to an elderly golden retriever was a small mirror which Lara hadn't noticed before. She supposed that she didn't look too bad, her hair was still dark with hardly any help, and she hadn't gone off the cut she had last week, which took her hair back to how it was before Poppy was born.

When she opened the door, there was no one there. Lara was struck by how quiet it was. Clapham High Street was only a hundred metres away, but for a moment it seemed as if the snowy cloud that had been sitting above London over the last couple of days had absorbed all sound. As a bus passed, a figure stepped over the rusty wire which divided Amanda's garden from her neighbour's.

'Lara,' said Archie.

Lara felt Amanda behind her. 'You remember Archie,

Lara,' she sniffed. 'Him next door. He's going to look at the house for me.'

In the kitchen Lara watched Archie arrange his heavy, navy worsted coat on the back of a chair. She had a dim recollection of meeting him at one of Amanda's parties. He was tall and slim and probably about 50, which made him about fifteen years older than Amanda. He was wearing a white shirt and a nicely cut navy suit and highly polished black shoes with fancy silver buckles. She thought that his partner – Megan? – was younger than all of them.

Archie sat himself down somewhat gingerly in Amanda's non-rocking rocking chair and stretched out his long legs. Snazzy yellow and green socks. 'We're looking forward,' he said to Amanda but catching Lara's eye as he spoke, 'to your Christmas party.'

'Oh, God, I'd forgotten about that,' said Amanda. 'Hang on, I thought that you and Meg had split up?'

'We have,' he replied, blushing, 'but now she and Paulo have also split up, so she's staying with me for a few weeks. She's buying a flat.'

Amanda nodded in approval. 'That's good of you, Archie.'

He shrugged as if to ask what else could he do. He looked around the kitchen and for a moment Lara saw it through his eyes. The worn-out kilims, the brass kettle with the missing spout, the upside-down colander lampshade, the floor-to-ceiling driftwood bookcase, the patch of crumbly brick in the wall, the rocking horse without a tail, the Welsh dresser on which Amanda had painted tiny silver stars, and under the window, the chipped William Morris-style tiles.

Archie nodded at the baking trays covered in fairy cakes on the table. 'You've been working hard,' he said to Amanda cheerily.

'Yes, it's all go here,' she replied, slumping heavily into the armchair and letting her eyes close.

Lara perched herself on the end of the chaise longue. 'I can't remember,' she said to Archie, 'do you have children?'

He gave her a look of infinite sadness. 'No, afraid not. We didn't really try, you know, when things were going well.'

'But they're not going well now?'

Archie put his hands together as if in prayer. 'I think I'm driving her mad. I've been living on my own for a couple of years. It's not easy having someone else in the house ... I mean,' he added, with a sad grin, 'when you get older.' He stood up and went over to the window. 'But if we hadn't got on, we wouldn't have been together for so long, would we?' He turned to look at Lara. 'There's no reason why we can't be friends.'

Lara thought that she ought to keep quiet. In her view the most that one could hope for on the ex-front was mutual toleration with the occasional smile if you're lucky. If there are children, you have to make an effort, that was obvious. Though perhaps not too much of an effort. She'd always thought that there was something sad about those ex-couples who remain cosily close to each other, who laugh like drains at ancient jokes and advise each other what to buy new partners at Christmas. Was it sad because they shouldn't have split up or was it sad because they're not facing up to what had happened? They were like those people who never really leave school. The kind who find any excuse to go back, whether to cheer on the old school from the side of the hockey pitch or football pitch or to attend endless dinners, who use not very amusing emails to organise gatherings in crowded pubs.

'What about you?' he was asking. 'How are you getting on with your ex? Jamie, isn't it?' How was she getting on? In that warm little kitchen, to the accompaniment of occasional shouts from the girls upstairs and curiously comforting mousey snoring sounds from Amanda, she told him more than she would have thought possible. That she hardly knew him made things easier. She was reminded of those occasions over the last year when she had unburdened herself to the wise men of North London at £180 an hour who knew the answer because there must be an answer, right? She began by saying that they tended to bicker. All would be going swimmingly and then a mistake would be made, usually in the form of a comment about the past, which meant, in effect, any comment about their time together. With your ex, she wanted to say, you should think of the past as a place surrounded by electric fences and guard dogs with a big neon sign saying *Don't even think about coming in here*. But as almost everything has a relation to the past, how was conversation with your ex possible without causing hurt and anger? Or should the two of them sit in companiable silence, perhaps occasionally stating mathematical propositions? She tried not to be too negative. She told Archie about meeting Jamie at court and how he had presented her with an unworkable plan for Poppy. She told him about their current arrangements, about how hard Jamie worked. She told him how at times last year she and Poppy had barely seen him from one week to another. When she set out the arguments for and against Jamie's plan, arguments which she now saw she had been preparing in the counsel's notebook of her mind, Archie listened carefully, every now and then asking her to clarify a point she had made. He was interested in her point of view, yes, but he was also interested in Jamie's point of view – not in order to find fault with it but because it was Jamie's point of view. Not a lawyer, then. What was rather lovely was that she felt no pressure to hurry up with what she was saying, no sense that he too wanted to talk about his problems.

Then he surprised her. 'What do they do on their Wednesday afternoons?'

'What do they do? His flat's not that near her school so they usually go to a café or the Krispy Kreme place in Raynes Park and talk about books.'

'Books?'

'Yes, Jamie has always read a lot of fiction and Poppy takes after him. She's just started *The Great Gatsby*.'

'That's good'

'Yes, I suppose it is.'

'Do you know what I think?' he said. 'I think that the three of you should go out somewhere, even for the day. Best to try somewhere new, no associations. There's no reason not to get on, none whatsoever.'

'I suppose we could,' she replied. 'But I'm not sure if it would work.'

'Worth trying,' he answered with a sad smile. 'My parents divorced when I was 7. They hated each other for the rest of their lives and took every opportunity to let my brother and me know it. Take it from me, you don't want to be like that.'

1st December

To: JamieAubrie@lawmail.com
From: Larissa@ChatsworthChambers.com

Hi Jamie

I've been thinking about what you said and have talked to Poppy. Why don't you have her for the next two weekends?

Regards Lara

2nd December

PENTECOST LOOKED UP FROM his screen as Lara came into the clerks' room and went over to her pigeonhole. She was wearing a black bobble hat and one of those padded black jackets that everyone wears in Italy. When she saw that there was nothing in it, she turned round. 'Morning, Pentecost. The Lewes brief for Friday? Didn't Mrs Sterne send it?'

'No. That's out, Lara.'

She frowned. 'It couldn't have settled? Surely not, the couple were at daggers drawn.'

Pentecost explained as best he could that Mrs Sterne the solicitor had been so annoyed at Lara's refusal to lower her brief fee that she'd instructed other counsel out of chambers.

Lara snatched off her hat as if to signal her astonishment. 'What? She wanted me to spend a day at Lewes County Court for £200 and not even pay my train fare?'

He took a deep breath. 'She said that you would be able to do other work on the train. Said that it wasn't right that her client should have to pay for that. "Facilitating that" was the expression she used.'

Lara laughed, and as she put her hat back on she gave him one of her radiant smiles. 'Pentecost, I think I'm in the wrong job. Don't you?'

'I think that the bar can be difficult,' he said, wanting to reassure her but not knowing quite what to say.

'When you mess up,' she said, walking towards the door

with an air of deep gloom, she was having one of her sudden changes of mood, 'they instruct you again. But when you do good work, they lose interest.'

'Then perhaps we shouldn't worry so much,' he said, hoping that he didn't sound patronising.

3rd December

WHEN ARCHIE CAUGHT SIGHT of the black Maserati parked outside his house, he assumed that Paulo had come to collect Meg and that after today he would never see her again. Ever. For a dark and gloomy moment the remarkably shiny car seemed to represent everything about its owner which he knew attracted Meg. It was sleek and it was new and it was doubtless worth lots of money. He pushed through the gate and walked up the snowy path wondering whose footprints he was looking at. Holding his breath, he opened the front door.

Meg was in the hall wearing her long, blue leather coat and holding one of his books. No sign of anyone else. 'Where's Paulo?'

She frowned. 'What do you mean?'

He opened the door and nodded towards the car. 'That's his, isn't it?' But as he spoke he knew that he had no idea what kind of car Paulo had. All he really knew about Paulo was that he lived on a smart estate in the Surrey Hills, that he had a pied-à-terre in Wimbledon, and that he was loved by Meg, his Meg of ten years who now pushed past him in her hurry to have a look at the shiny car.

She shut the front door firmly and said, without trying terribly hard to hide her disappointment, 'No, it's not one of Paulo's cars. I don't know where you got that idea from.'

Archie felt that he could breathe again. 'Sorry, I was confused ... but why are you wearing your coat?'

'We're going out. Don't you remember? We've got to be in the village in half an hour. I'm measuring up.'

'The village?'

'Wimbledon Village.'

'Why do you call it "the village?"'

She shrugged her narrow shoulders. 'Everyone else does.'

'Not when they live in Clapham.'

'I don't live in Clapham, Archie,' she said, a little too slowly, and with a little too much of a sympathetic expression for his liking. 'I'm just staying with you for a while,' she added as she started to look at her phone.

Archie had found Wimbledon Village a less than impressive place. Last Saturday, he and Meg had eaten croissants in a chi-chi café run by languid long-legged waitresses with perfect teeth who talked to each other in clipped accents about the Maldives when they should have been serving customers. Nor was life much faster outside. Back in the car, they found themselves crawling behind a line of horses, which had amused Meg as much as it had annoyed him. 'I like,' she said with a giggle, 'their traffic-calming measures.' He teased her by holding his hand over the horn.

'You'll make them bolt,' she said as she grabbed his arm.

'Suddenly, you're an expert on horses.'

'Be good, Archie.'

But now she was waving her phone at him as if he had never seen it before, which was strange given that it was rarely out of her hands. 'Look,' she said, 'an email from Toby.'

'Who's Toby?'

Meg sighed in that theatrical way she'd picked up at the Surrey Hills Amateur Dramatic Society. 'The estate agent. You know that. Why are you asking? He says I need to exchange by Christmas.'

'Exchange what?'

She glared at him. 'Don't be difficult.'

Archie did his best to look unconcerned. 'That won't be a problem,' he said with a little shake of his head.

She narrowed her eyes and peered at him. She knew him so well. He couldn't hide a thing from her. 'You're sure? If we don't exchange, the seller will put my flat back on the market.'

'Quite sure,' said Archie as he took the book from her hand and put it back on the shelf where it belonged. 'You know,' he said, making sure that the book was in line with his other books on the tragedy of Brexit, 'I wish you wouldn't tidy up.'

Not for the first time, she ignored him. 'Archie, why don't we go to Surrey tomorrow? There's a café in Shalford which overlooks the green. They do lovely bacon sandwiches there.'

'Meg, you want to go to Shalford because you might bump into your ex,' he said, sensing the absurdity of his giving such advice. 'You really do not want to think like that. I'm not here to advise you…'

'But you will,' she said sadly. 'Anyway, you're wrong, I think Paulo's in Australia.'

'So he's on the other side of the world.'

'I do know where Australia is.'

'I didn't mean it like that. But do we have to go to Wimbledon? Isn't it a bit early to measure up?'

Meg looked at him angrily and walked into the kitchen where she switched on her coffee machine which, apart from her three suitcases of clothes, was just about the only thing she'd brought from Paulo's. She carefully inserted a pod and pulled the lever down so hard that Archie was surprised it didn't come off in her hand. 'You know very well I want that flat,' she said. 'That's why we made the agreement, the one you signed, the one you dated. It wouldn't have worked without me.'

She meant of course the property management business. He had his surveying practice but the property management was something else. The two of them had managed around a hundred flats in South Kensington and thirty or forty in Earls Court. And Meg was right, she had made it work. Since she'd left, things had never been the same. In fact they'd been pretty dreadful. She had always been a complete natural. Landlords wanted her to manage their properties and tenants wanted to pay her their rent. Everyone loved her, everything ran smoothly. She even dealt with the contractors, which of course was how she had met Paulo, the most popular interior designer in Dorking. Given the huge contribution she had made to the development of the business, it had seemed right to Archie to give her a share of its worth. He had thought that negotiations would go on for ages, but in November, not that long before her bust up with Paulo, they agreed on a sum which she now planned to use to pay the deposit on a flat.

'Meg, Meg, I'm not going back on what we agreed, I'm just a bit tired, that's all.'

'Sorry, Archie, I didn't mean to raise my voice,' she said as she touched him on the upper part of his left arm, the second touch in a year. He should put notches on the coffee machine before he lost count.

'That's alright. Suppose it can't be easy. But I'm not sure why you want to go as far as Wimbledon. I've always thought it a bit of a dump.'

'Lots of reasons,' she said, cheerful again. 'For a start, I want to be near my book club friends.'

'You could ask around,' he said, always one for a practical answer. 'There's bound to be a book club near here.'

'It's not like looking for a public toilet, Archie. Joining the group was bad enough, it really frightened me.'

'That's because you hadn't read a book in years.'

'Well, I wasn't in a club,' she said, laughing.

'I could come with you,' he said. 'They'd have me, wouldn't they?'

'We're all women.'

'I could dress up.'

Meg laughed and Archie remembered how he'd missed that laugh. He found himself wondering if his new friend Lara would find his silly voices funny. Probably not. Wasn't she a bit serious? He had a vague idea that she'd been a junior research fellow in psychology before switching to law. Hadn't he seen a copy of the *London Review of Books* sticking out of her bag?

'Some of them are quite intellectual, Archie. There's this girl Susie...'

'I was at Cambridge, you know.'

'You did engineering,' said Meg, 'and then you were chucked out.'

'Sent down, Megan, I was sent down...but it's not just the distance – you have to admit that the flat's very expensive for what it is.'

She saw through that at once. 'But I thought the business was doing well? You've got Benedict now.'

'Benedict, bless him, is not half as good as you are.' He didn't know how much to tell her. He disliked the idea of keeping things from Meg but he didn't want to admit that the business was not exactly booming. He was beginning to dread opening his emails in the morning as more and more landlords were giving him notice and more and more leaseholders were opting either to buy their freeholds or to manage the flats themselves. Half the letters were from solicitors, which was bad enough, and more than a few were complaints about Benedict, complaints which he'd so far ignored. Looking at Meg as she searched on her iPhone for another email from Toby, he wondered if he should explain that he was having to sell one of his own flats to finance the deal. But what if he couldn't sell the flat quickly? What if the tenant refused to move out? He would have to pay her to go, he accepted that. But what if she dug her heels in or asked for silly money?

4th December

LARA, SITTING ON A window seat in Georgie's kitchen watching her friend tap out a message, found herself thinking how she would describe the scene to Archie. The slate floor, the marble working surfaces, the stainless steel retro-style fridge and, through the window, the lights flickering on the other side of Clapham Common. What would she say about Georgie? She would mention her pale freckly skin, her cupid lips, her red hair in its spiky sub-Aladdin Sane cut, and her slim almost gamine figure which hadn't changed since bar school. How did she stay looking so young? It helped that she had a cleaner and a gardener and someone to pick up her little ones from school. And all those holidays. What about her voice? A Belfast accent, yes, a tone somewhat lower than most women's voices, a voice which at times seemed to reverberate around the somewhat cavernous kitchen.

Georgie was looking at her. 'I've been thinking about what you said the other day. I'd really like to represent you. I don't do much children work but I'm sure I could manage it.'

'That's incredibly kind. But I wonder if I should find someone who doesn't know him?'

'God, no,' said Georgie. 'Knowing him will be an advantage.'

'You don't think that I should do it myself?'

'That's always a bad idea,' she said. 'Look, you needn't worry. He won't stand a chance. This is what we should do ….'

But Lara was beginning to have her doubts about the

wisdom of a fight, and the more Georgie spoke the stronger those doubts became. She'd seen too many instances where litigation about contact or money had damaged the man's relationship with the children. She knew feckless men who were not interested in their children and damn them to hell. But she also knew men who were so bitter about the public beating-up they'd received from their ex that their relationship with their children had suffered. If you humiliate someone, you never really know what the consequences will be. Quite simply, if she made Jamie hate her, would he really stay so close to Poppy who had her mother's brown hair and brown eyes? And yet how could she agree that he could look after Poppy for half the week when he plainly could not look after Poppy for half the week?

Georgie pulled open a drawer. 'I still don't understand,' she said, 'why he's suddenly so keen to see more of her.'

'Nor do I,' said Lara. She had given that some thought. When they'd split up the previous year, they had agreed that Jamie would see Poppy every other weekend and every Wednesday afternoon, and by and large that is what had happened. At the time, he'd seemed perfectly content with the arrangement. She wondered if Christmas had something to do with his change of view. His firm closed down for Christmas, and doubtless he was thinking of all the days he would otherwise have to spend by himself.

'I wouldn't be surprised if this was about working less,' said Georgie, picking up a knife. 'That happens to middle-aged men, you know. They lose interest in work. Don't blame yourself, Lara, it's a design fault.'

'He's talking about doing less, not giving up altogether.'

'That's how it starts,' replied Georgie, feeling the sharpness of the knife with her thumb. 'You wait – in a couple of years, he'll be doing a day a week, and by the time he's 50, it'll be the occasional evening at the Citizens' Advice Bureau when he's bored. Giles is just as bad.'

'I heard that,' said Giles as he came into the kitchen carrying a pipe in one hand and holding a large book in the other. For a split second Lara wondered if Giles was going to a fancy-dress party. Giles the rich estate agent always dressed like a rich estate agent but now he was wearing round tortoiseshell faux 1930s glasses, a tweed sports jacket with worn leather patches on the elbows, an artfully crumpled red and green bow tie, baggy grey flannels and heavy brown brogues. He sat down on the stool next to Lara and began to flick through his book as Georgie stared at him. 'They'll be here in an hour,' she growled. 'I thought you were going to make a pudding?'

'Don't order me around,' he said without looking up. 'Where's Anaïs?'

'She's upstairs giving the girls a lesson. You'll start, will you?'

He waited a moment before replying. 'When I'm ready.' He carefully turned a page with his long fingers.

'Giles,' said Georgie, 'Lara's here.' She rolled her eyes at Lara. 'I'll go and see how the girls are getting on.'

'So how are you, Giles?' asked Lara as Georgie slammed the door behind her.

Giles sniffed. 'So-so.'

'Anaïs won't mind Poppy being there?'

'I'm sure she won't.' He closed his book and looked at Lara with his somewhat hooded green eyes. 'She's a marvellous teacher, just marvellous, though she drives Georgie mad. But there again, everyone drives Georgie mad.' He stood up. 'As you heard, I'm supposed to be making the pudding. It's figs and honey, her favourite. By the way, I apologise for her not being on great form. She has a trial on Monday which she's dreading.'

'I know the feeling.'

'But it's not just that. She doesn't like my going to philosophy classes, that's the problem of the moment. She says that estate agents shouldn't be doing that. She says it wasn't part of the deal. I don't remember that. I don't remember the priest mentioning philosophy. The fact is,' he said as he fumbled with his pipe, 'the classes are really important to me. It's alright for Georgie, but I've been selling houses since I left school and all the time I've known: this isn't me.'

'She's probably worried about you.'

'She thinks I exist because I sell. Yes, I sell therefore I am. I wonder what that is in Latin? I suppose I could look it up on what I believe is called 'the internet.' Giles's estate agency had been using the internet for thirty years.

He peered inquisitively at Lara. 'Have you ever tried to believe something that would make you happy?'

'More than once.'

'It doesn't work, does it? You can't choose to believe. Either you do or you don't. That was Hume's view, of course.'

'Of course. For example?'

He looked towards the window. 'That Georgie still loves me,' he said. 'I can no more believe that than I can believe that life is an illusion. I remind myself of the years we have spent together, I remember the beautiful places we have visited, I look at our children, I think of her sleeping, and for a while, when I really put my mind to it, I can think that she loves me. But as soon as I'm distracted, as soon as I talk to friends, or play backgammon, the idea appears ridiculous. Do you know what I sometimes do? I pretend that we're exes. I find that that allows us to get on. I am like a mystic who finds himself imagining rejecting God in order to feel closer to Him. Really, how crazy is that?'

'Giles,' said Lara, touching the sleeve of his jacket and feeling its roughness, 'you're wrong, I'm sure she loves you.'

'She's so aggressive,' he said, shaking his head in disbelief.

It was true that Georgie had precisely that reputation, which at the bar, as Lara knew, takes some doing. It was rumoured that she had once reduced her Head of Chambers to tears and that at Oxford she had kicked a policeman. Or was it the other way round?

Now she was at the door. 'Did he offer you a glass of wine?'

'I'd love one.'

She bustled in. 'And did he tell you his news?'

'I've applied for a course at Oxford,' said Giles proudly. 'I should know by Christmas.'

Georgie snorted. 'It's your Christmas wish, isn't it Giles? We all know what we want, don't we? My Christmas wish is to have a normal husband again, though I can't see that happening.'

Giles sighed. 'I look on Oxford as my spiritual home.'

'How can it be your home if you've never been there?' snapped Georgie.

Giles was surprised. 'Darling, don't you remember the weekend we had in the hotel near Blenheim?' He began to dig out his pipe with what looked like a bent paper clip.

'Oh, yes,' said Georgie, looking at Giles sadly. 'But who would pay for you to go to Oxford? And what about your work? I thought I only had the children to worry about.'

'The truth conditions to that proposition are not in place,' said Giles, winking at Lara.

'That means I'm talking rubbish,' translated Georgie as Giles began to fill his pipe. 'In fact,' she added, 'I'm more worried about the children than I am about his work. They've hardly brought any friends home over the last few weeks. You know why? They're embarrassed. Look at him. He looks like a 1930s Oxford don.'

'I read an interesting book on truth last week, Georgie,' said Giles, using his thumb to press down tobacco into his pipe. 'It's by Simon Blackburn. A little old but still, ah, relevant. Would you like it for Christmas, darling?'

She ignored him. 'The children don't understand what he goes on about,' she said. 'You can't expect them to. After all, he doesn't understand what he's saying himself half the time. He used to talk about how he'd sold this or that house but now he wants to prove the existence of the external world. Prove the existence of Clapham? He's been selling the external world on 4 per cent commission for the last twenty years. That's all the proof he needs.'

'Don't take any notice of her,' advised Giles as he lit his pipe with a shaking hand. 'At first it feels rude, but after a while you get used to it.'

Lara said, 'May I have that glass of wine, please? And could it be quite large?'

'Of course you can,' said Georgie. 'Giles, pass me the corkscrew, will you?'

Lara watched as Giles clenched his pipe in his teeth and yanked open the drawer.

'Do be careful, Giles,' advised Georgie as she reached over and picked up a bottle.

Giles passed the corkscrew to Georgie. 'Here we are, dearest.'

She peered closely at him and frowned. 'What's that on your face?'

'It could be love, it could be hatred.'

'You've been eating the effing figs.'

'No I bloody have not.'

'Do you want me to open it?' asked Lara, feeling that if she didn't have a drink she would surely die.

'Allow me,' said Giles, snatching both bottle and corkscrew from Georgie. He stabbed in the corkscrew and gave it a couple of ferocious twists before pulling out the cork as if he was pulling out Georgie's heart.

'Oh, Giles, this smoke,' shouted Georgie, waving her thin arms around as if she was on the flight deck of an aircraft carrier. 'You'll have to go outside this evening, I'm just not having it.' She stood up and went over to the bookshelf opposite the fridge where she took down a battered old copy of *French Provincial Cooking*. She peered at the shelf again and picked out a book with a shiny red cover which she held up between thumb and forefinger as she wrinkled her nose. It was called *On Certainty*. 'What's this effing rubbish doing in my effing kitchen?'

Giles pointed a knife at her. 'I've been looking for that for ages. You didn't ask if you could borrow it. Give it to me. Now.'

Lara watched Georgie slide the book along the marble work surface towards Giles who stopped it with his elbow. He scowled at Georgie who picked up an onion and cut it in half. A moment later, she swore loudly. Lara looked up to see her holding out her hand from which blood was slowly dripping. Giles took a couple of steps closer towards her. 'Not enough attention, darling?' He caught Lara's eye. 'What it is to be married to a member of the bar. Never a dull moment.'

Lara thought Georgie was going to slap him but if that was her intention she didn't have a chance because Giles put his arms around her and kissed her. 'Look the other way everyone,' he said.

Georgie pushed him away, though not roughly. 'Why don't you do something sensible like find me a plaster?'

So Giles went to the cupboard on the other side of the kitchen and came back with a first-aid box about the size of a cottage hospital. 'Here, let me look at it,' he said, taking hold of Georgie's hand. 'You poor old thing. This should do.' He wrapped a plaster around her finger.

'Welcome to the mad house, Lara,' said Georgie.

5th December

To: Larissa@ChatsworthChambers.com
From: Pentecost@ChatsworthChambers.com

Mr Luba called about the brief fee for next week's trial. He says that the client does not have much money. He also says that if you do this one for free he is sure that he will be able to give you lots of work next year. Please let me know how much you want me to charge.

Regards
Pentecost Burnett

Practice Manager

6th December

To: Archie1939@easymail.com
From: Megan88@fabmail.com

Archie, I am seeing my solicitor this afternoon. He says that we should talk things through in case anything goes wrong. I think he means by that: in case you can't raise the money for the flat.

By the way, please lend me £2000 as the solicitor wants that on account.

Meg

7th December

'O PARADISO,' SANG CARUSO.

Lara had been at home preparing an Advice on a matrimonial dispute for most of the afternoon without making much progress. Caruso hadn't helped. Hunting for her stapler in the kitchen drawer she'd found one of Jamie's stray CDs, and out of curiosity, and perhaps out of a desire for something to sweeten the bitterness of the fight, she'd slipped the disc into the player on the middle shelf of their now almost empty bookcase. That she should be playing opera was a surprise: she and opera had never really clicked. Her attitude had always been that she could take it or leave it and for the most part she'd left it. However hard Jamie tried to persuade her to like it, there was part of her which rejected it. Her brain. Opera, she used to say, without claiming originality, is so irrational. When people meet, they don't sing, and when people die of horrible lung diseases, they sing even less. She knew of course that the composers and librettists aren't stupid, and she knew that this was about her and not opera … but that didn't change the fact that people don't sing. Now, however, Caruso's voice seemed to change everything, and the fact that the recording was made in a hotel room in Milan in 1904 added to its crackly magic: he was singing to her from another world. As she waded through a fat lever ach file containing a lot of unhappiness and a lot of bank statements, she found herself looking forward to telling Jamie about her discovery.

Poppy would be home in a moment and then she would

have to stop. On balance, though, it was easier to work at home than work in chambers where since her eviction she had had to share a rather small room with the very junior tenants and the pupils, all of whom were at least ten years younger than she was. They seemed to spend one half of their lives looking forward to holidays and the other half looking back, often, she'd noticed, with a tinge of regret for doing this rather than that. None of them were very friendly, and she knew why that was.

When she reached the bottom of the page, she saved what she had written, pushed back her chair and went into the kitchen where she began to put the breakfast things away. But the miasma of loathing which her client felt for her ex, and her ex felt for her client, seemed to go with her. She found herself asking how long she could continue with matrimonial work. What was it doing to her, dealing day in day out with such anger? How much had that contributed to the break-up? Or was she being unreasonable? The chances were that the couple in the brief were perfectly ordinary people whose relationship had broken down, and who were then driven mad by the separation and the subsequent fight organised by the lawyers. Time and time again she had seen decent people behave like monsters. A woman she had advised last year, someone who spent Christmas feeding down and outs and every Saturday afternoon working in her local Oxfam shop, had her husband's whippet put down when it suffered a minor graze. Last week her client, whom she and her instructing solicitor had thought perfectly charming, claimed that he had 'lost' his wife's old laptop containing thousands of photos of his stepchildren. No family solicitor would encourage such acts, of course, but their bills did little to settle already troubled souls. When chambers held parties for instructing solicitors, you could always tell who the family solicitors were: the ones with the most expensive suits and the most expensive handbags.

But it's too easy to blame the lawyers, she thought, as she slammed the dishwasher door shut, the madness comes from within. When she and Jamie had split up, she would sometimes in her unhappiness see in this kitchen nothing but the subjects of arguments. The sandstone floor was Jamie's choice; she had wanted grey slate. She had found the copper lamps now hanging over the wooden work surfaces; he had wanted spotlights. The Quaker-style cupboards were his choice; she had wanted another style, she couldn't remember which. She shivered now, thinking how at times in those bleak and angry months parts of the house which he had chosen seemed to be out of place, to be ill-fitted, as if the house was dividing into two elements, as if their home was coming apart. How mad was that?

That she now saw the madness was surely progress. The things she was looking at in the kitchen might have been the subject of conflicting choices but they were also their resolution. That was why, when she was away and missing home, she would still find herself thinking of this room with its pencil marks on the wall where they had measured Poppy's height over the years, and the Pissarro picture of Upper Norwood in the snow which they all liked, and the somewhat lugubrious photograph of poor D.H. Lawrence in his nice cream suit which Jamie had pinned on the dado rail, and the snapshots which were always falling off the fridge door, and the gap in the skirting board where Jamie had seen the mouse which he said was a rat but which certainly wasn't.

She was putting the milk in the fridge when she heard Poppy's key in the door.

'You've forgotten, haven't you?' said Poppy as she dropped her coat on the sofa instead of hanging it up in the hall.

'Forgotten what?'

Poppy shook her head in disbelief and took a glass from the cupboard. When she walked towards the sink, Lara thought for the first time in ages how like Jamie she looked. They were both tall and she had his slightly awkward way of moving.

As Poppy sipped her water and leaned back against the fridge, a photo fell. 'Tomorrow, Mum. Inset day. Hampton Court.'

'Yes, I know.'

'The car, Mum. It's in the garage.'

'Yes, I know.' There were times when Poppy talked to her as if she was a complete idiot.

'We'll go by train.'

'Not the train,' groaned Poppy. 'Can't we go with Dad?'

'There's nothing wrong with the train. Anyway, I'm sure he's working.'

'He's not, he's using up holidays.'

'You haven't asked him, have you?'

'Yes, I have.'

'Alright, I'll call him.'

Poppy waited a moment and looked at Lara oddly. 'He said that when he met you at court, he gave you a book to give me.'

'Oh, God, he did. I'm sorry, I think it's in chambers.'

'You think? You didn't deliberately "lose" it?'

'Of course not, darling. It's in chambers. Promise.'

8th December

WEARING THE GREY BRUAR jacket she'd bought him for his birthday last year, Jamie was driving the Porsche the way he usually drove the Porsche: resting his hands on the top of the steering wheel and going far too bloody fast. He was doing 60 on a road where the limit was 50, 60 with Poppy in the car. As they began the descent after the New Malden underpass, the road felt more like a runway than road, and for a moment Lara had the sense that they might take off into the blue winter sky.

For most of the time, he'd been speaking to Anaïs whilst using headphones. Every now and then he would glance at Lara and raise his eyebrows, as if he had forgotten that only he could hear what Anaïs was saying. It was obvious to Lara that he found Anaïs attractive. You don't spend fifteen years with someone without being able to detect the signs, though quite what those were was more difficult to say. But she sensed that he wanted to keep the relationship with Anaïs private, that he would let her know in his own time.

'I think that we might as well issue,' he was saying to Anaïs as Lara gazed politely out of the window and pretended that she wasn't listening. There had been times when she had found the way that his voluntary work followed him on weekends and holidays distinctly annoying. But now she had been apart from him she could see that as something to complain about, it didn't even register, that complaining about that would say more about her than about him.

'You can ask,' he said, 'your phone provider to block those calls. Anyway, speak to you later.'

'These lanes,' she found herself saying, 'are horribly narrow.'

Jamie laughed. 'You mean slow down.'

'No I don't. If I'd wanted to say slow down, I'd have said slow down.'

'Is that right?'

'Yes.'

'Ok.'

'You do know the way, don't you?'

'Of course I do. It's not that far from your Dad. I could find it with my eyes closed.

She wouldn't have him rewrite the past. 'But you always avoided trips to see Dad.'

'Nonsense.'

'Oh come on, Jamie,' she said, glancing behind her and seeing that Poppy was wearing her headphones as she always did now when the three of them were in the car together, as if she didn't want to hear her mother and father talk. 'Your excuse was either opera or work or traffic. I'm sure that you once mentioned the possibility of terrorism in Cobham.'

'Your imagination knows no bounds.'

'Jamie, for you, Surrey always seemed to be the hardest word.'

'That was my joke!'

'Oh, for God's sake.'

She found herself thinking of their trip to Brighton almost exactly a year ago. She had known that the memory of that trip would come back to her today. The decision at breakfast that they would go. Zooming along under a gorgeous blue sky. Playing *I spy.* Talking about her childhood. Impersonating herself telling the class she wanted to be a judge. Listening to Jamie talking about the music he had heard as a child. Glancing at him and thinking that, if she had a Tardis, she would set the controls for his childhood. Insisting that they play *First one to see the sea*, with the loser having to buy the ice creams. Reaching the top of the South Downs and 15 minutes later, Poppy shouting, 'The sea!'

On the pier she and Poppy had left Jamie on a bench with only the seagulls for company. Poppy dragged her into an amusement arcade where they played those machines where the coins piled up until it appeared that in a moment all the riches of Brighton would be theirs. 'Just one more! Look, over here! Where can we change the money? I can't believe we won't win… .' After that they had walked past candyfloss stalls and hot dog stalls and sweet stalls and watched a fisherman at the end of the pier cast his line into the sea before spending 5 minutes looking for a bracelet for Poppy.

When they'd come back, Jamie had been lost in thought, miles away he was. She and Poppy had continued the conversation about climate change they'd begun when they'd watched the fisherman. As she'd thought he would, Jamie soon joined in. His viewpoint was contrary to theirs but she'd resisted the temptation to argue back and contented herself with the occasional gentle prod at the weaker parts of his arguments. Then Poppy had wanted an ice cream so Jamie had given her his cagoule and went off to play his hunter-gatherer role, which on balance Lara preferred to his climate-specialist one.

She remembered feeling the warmth of the sun on her face and listening to snippets of conversation from people walking past and the cries of the seagulls, now above her, now further away, and in the background the sound of the fruit machines and electronic gunfire. How foolish they were to argue! Their arguments were so embarrassingly banal, so suburban. But they didn't have to agree about everything, it was a mistake to think that. Next summer, they would go to Greece for two weeks, they would spend family time in the sun together, then *everything* would come right. How could she not have insisted on family time?

Buzz.

Poppy had lifted Jamie's iPhone from the cagoule pocket. 'Dad's received a text.'

'Has he, darling? You know our rule about not reading other people's texts.'

She'd looked up to see Jamie standing before them with three ice creams. How blue his eyes were! How handsome her lover was! She'd given him a smile that said: *Sorry for being grumpy over the last few months. Sorry for arguing about nothing. We are so lucky. You are my man. I love you.*

But Jamie was looking at Poppy who was reading a text on his iPhone with an expression on her face which Lara would never forget.

'Sorry, Mum. Mum, I'm so sorry.'

She'd snatched the phone from Poppy's hand.

The journey home. The periods of silence. She and Jamie at different times and in different ways trying to convince Poppy that the text had no significance, that it was as silly and as inconsequential as most texts are. Inside, she was raging. That Poppy should see desire for her father set out like that. That Poppy, even accidentally, should have been able to play some part in whatever happened. It really disgusted her.

After supper, Poppy had gone to bed early and without any fuss, as if she'd known that her parents needed privacy.

Lara hadn't wanted to eat anything and nor had Jamie. They'd each poured themself a glass of wine before sitting on sofas at right angles to the smouldering log-burner. On the opposite wall was their floor-to-ceiling bookcase, half of which had been taken up with Jamie's opera CDs.

What made everything worse, Lara thought as she watched Jamie check his phone, was that the day had been going so well. She was reminded of a time last year in court when she had been listening to the judgment and everything had seemed to be going her way. Her witnesses had performed as they should have performed. The law and the facts had been on her side. Her preparation and cross-examination had been adequate, and the judge had seemed to like her submissions. But then she'd realised that she had it wrong. Either the judge had changed his mind in the middle of giving judgment or he had praised her witnesses only to appear even-handed. Whatever the reason, he had finally found for her opponent.

What also made it worse was Jamie's denial.

'I know it didn't look good.'

'No?'

'You mustn't get the wrong idea.'

'I see.'

'Emma's a very old friend. She's been very unhappy.'

'I'm sorry to hear that.'

'Her husband's left her.'

'When you made that call in the garden last week, was that her?'

'What call?'

'How many calls do you make in the garden?'

He frowned. 'No, that was Gina, she's a trainee.'

'Trainee solicitor or trainee girlfriend?'

'She's running a marathon, she wants sponsorship.'

'Odd that you never mentioned that.'

'Why should I?'

'And is Mary also running a marathon? I seem to recall that she had long legs.'

'Mary?'

'You know, the one before me. Your ex. Or perhaps she's your ex-ex? Tall with black hair.'

'Lara, I went out with her 15 years ago.'

'Jamie, you took her out for supper last summer.'

'We like to keep in touch.'

'You did take her out.'

'Yes.'

'You know what this is like?' asked Lara.

'Being in the witness box?'

'No, it's like that programme you listen to on Saturday afternoons as you lie on the sofa.'

'I get tired.'

'The one where they play a number of opera recordings and then select the best one.'

'Building a Library. It's not just operas but symphonies, chamber music, solo instrumental works, song cycles, oratorios…'

'I wonder who would win out of your women? Would I even be on the shortlist?'

'Lara, I'm having a sense of humour failure. Please shut up.'

'There's Mary who's from a different era, that has its own attractions.'

'Lara.'

'Then there's the trainee, who clearly has loads of energy.'

'Lara.'

'And Emma, your very old friend. If nothing else, Emma has a great sense of timing. That's important, don't you think?'

'Stop this.'

'Finally, there's Lara. She seemed so impressive once. But now? Tastes change.'

'Please.'

'I can see that it's going to be a very difficult choice.'

'Actually, they nearly always say that on the programme. I suppose that at a certain point the recommendation has a subjective element.'

'Is that right? How very interesting. Perhaps that will apply to your choice, too?'

'Lara, that's enough. The text was just a silly flirty joke.'

'A silly flirty joke.'

'Don't be difficult, Lara.'

'I mustn't be difficult.'

'Look, I know it's really embarrassing.'

'When did you last see her?'

'Wednesday. I had a cup of coffee with her, there's a new place on Lavender Hill.'

'How was it?'

'Not easy, she's seriously depressed.'

'I mean the café. I know that good coffee is one of the things that's really important to you.'

'Lara.'

'Jamie? Or perhaps I should call you James, I've never called you James, that's your real name, isn't it? I am sure that I saw that somewhere. I know, I know. Poppy's birth certificate. Memory. What is stranger than memory?'

'Lara.'

'Larissa.'

'Lara.'

'Larissa.'

'Lara.'

'James. Everything else about you is unreal. So let's hold onto that, shall we?'

'It didn't mean anything.'

'Why were you meeting her for coffee? In the new café on Lavender Hill which may or may not meet with your approval, a fact which for some reason you are unwilling to vouchsafe. I think that you may be quite a secretive person, James.'

'Please do be not like this.'

'Funny that you did not mention that you were meeting up with her. When I say that it was funny, I don't mean that it was funny ha ha. I mean odd.'

'I didn't want to make you jealous.'

'And why should it have made me jealous?'

'There was no reason for you to be jealous.'

'Then why should you have worried?'

'People get the wrong idea.'

'I'm *people* am I? Wow. But why would I get the wrong idea?'

'I suppose because of appearances.'

'So there was no need to hide what you were doing, to creep about in the cover of darkness?'

'You're being ridiculous. She's just a friend, nothing's happened.'

'Forgive me, Jamie, for doubting your word, but sending a text like that is not, I think, common when the recipient is *just a friend.* I can't remember sending a text like that to Amanda or Georgie or to Giles …'

'I suppose it was ironic.'

'Ironic?'

'Jokey.'

'Jokey?'

'Nothing's happened.'

'Nothing's happened?'

'Stop repeating everything, Lara. You sound like some minimalist opera.'

'How many times have you seen her in the last month?'

'I don't know.'

'I'm sure you do.'

'Three?'

'When are you are going to see her again.'

'Tomorrow, actually.'

After this, she'd thought, *he's still seeing her tomorrow. He's still seeing her tomorrow. He's still fucking seeing her tomorrow.*

'Are you alright, Lara?'

'No, I'm not alright, Jamie. If you must know, I've never felt less alright.'

'I'm sorry.'

'It's not a matter of being sorry or not sorry. It's quite simple, Jamie: I was wrong about you. I thought you were my rock but you are nothing of the sort.'

'You're being ridiculous, this is not all about you.'

'I know. But I think that you should go anyway.'

'Go?'

'Yes. I can say it in Russian if you like, or in Italian, or in French. Even in German.'

'What? You're kidding? Because of a text?'

'No, not because of a text. You don't have time to see Poppy and me but you *do* have time to see Emily.'

'Emma.'

'Emma then.'

'When we *do* have time together, we argue.'

'We argue, do we?'

'The fact is, Lara, you just love arguing, it's what you're really good at. That's why you ended up at the bar.'

'I did not end up at the bar, Jamie. I chose my profession.'

'It was a good choice. You were born for it.'

'We don't just argue, that's unfair.'

'You see what I mean?'

'Now *you're* being ridiculous.'

'I'm ridiculous, am I?'

'If you won't face up to what has happened, then yes.'

'Lara, I'm fed up with your cold unforgiving logic.'

'It's not my logic that's unforgiving Jamie, it's me.'

'Thanks.'

'I think that you should go.'

'I think so, too.'

***

It was when they were buying the tickets that Poppy remembered that sometimes her parents would argue for fun. Her dad told the man behind the desk they wanted a family ticket and her mum said that they didn't.

'I think we do,' insisted Dad, with that pretend-stern face which appeared at such moments. 'One family ticket, please.'

'No,' said Mum. 'I'm paying.'

She poked him in the ribs, which, though it could be classed as disrespectful, struck Poppy as a good sign. 'My treat. Two adults and one child please. It's cheaper, Jamie.'

'Absolutely not,' he said, in his I'm-digging-my-heels-in voice that she hadn't heard for ages. 'This is on me. It's only less if you don't pay the voluntary donation.'

'What's that?' she asked, for a moment not knowing something.

'Look, there.' He pointed with an air of satisfaction to a notice which explained that the Palace was seeking to raise a million pounds for the repair of the Tijou Screen in the Privy Garden.

'There's also a voluntary donation on the family ticket, sir,' said the large unshaven man behind the counter, trying to be helpful.

'Doesn't sound very voluntary to me,' answered Mum with a nice smile, as if she wanted him to join in the game.

Poppy stepped forward. 'It says there that the family ticket includes two children. We could have brought Jess.'

Mum answered immediately. 'It's not quite right to say that the ticket *includes* two children, darling. It's not as if they are given to you with the ticket.'

'Lara.'

'The ticket,' she continued, as Dad put on his Mum-in-court face, '*allows* you to bring two children. But however much we love her, Jess isn't part of the family, so we could hardly bring her with us on a family ticket.'

'That would be alright, Madam,' said the man as he glanced anxiously at the queue which had formed behind them. 'Families are so mixed-up nowadays, we can't really ask who the children belong to.'

In a way, thought Poppy, as they headed for the Royal Kitchens, it was ok that they argued because everyone knows that real families argue. And it wasn't as if they argued like the families in the books she used to read before she discovered Francis Scott Fitzgerald. They didn't throw things at each other and afterwards take drugs in her bedroom. When they were arguing at the ticket desk, they both had smiles on their faces. But how weird was that?

The kitchens were cold, and Poppy shivered despite the fact that she was wearing her red ski-jacket, the one they'd together bought her in Italy. They moved through a group of French teenagers towards a huge fireplace where a servant, or probably an actor playing a servant, was turning a piece of meat on a spit. On the other side of the room were baskets of carrots, cauliflowers, sprouts and parsnips. She could tell that the vegetables were real because some of them were beginning to turn black.

On leaving the kitchens, they decided to look for the Royal Apartments and after wandering around for 10 minutes, they found themselves in a courtyard where above them a dark cloud was framed by the red brick walls. They walked over worn paving slabs, worn down by ghosts, said Dad, he sometimes spoke to her as if she were still about 10, to the middle of the courtyard where they saw that there were two doors to choose from. They took the one on the left and passed down a corridor full of signs for toilets for the disabled. When they reached the end, they turned right and, after bypassing the servants' kitchen, came to a different courtyard with the same red bricks and after that they went through a door and along another corridor. Then there was a doorway so small that Dad had to duck his head and they were back in the kitchen where the man was still turning the spit.

'The thing about Hampton Court,' said Mum, 'is that the maze is the only place where you don't get lost.'

'I'll ask someone,' said Dad helpfully.

Mum shook her head. 'There's a plan on the ticket.'

'What's wrong with asking?' he asked, sighing.

'There's no need,' she replied in her confident way. 'But don't worry, Poppy, we're not arguing. We're reaching a mutual decision. That's right, isn't it Jamie?'

'If you say so,' he said, with a nice smile.

'Don't you think it's like a fairy palace, Poppy?' said Mum. 'I can imagine a prince riding down the drive.'

'For God's sake,' said Poppy.

'What about asking this servant?' suggested Mum.

So Dad asked a wobble-chinned servant who sent them

through a gateway and up some stairs where they caught a glimpse of the gardens and a lake which seemed to go on forever. Poppy watched as a horse and open carriage slowly progressed around the edge of the lawn. A flock of doves took to the air as the horse approached. On the path below, an elderly woman lent on her walking stick, and when she dropped a newspaper into a litter bin, her long turquoise and gold sari fluttered in the wind. Sitting on a bench behind her, facing the lawn and the dark green trees, two men were sharing food from a Tesco's carrier bag. The sun glinted on the metal foil which one passed to the other.

On Dad's suggestion, they tagged along for a while with a group being shown around by a man wearing a black hat, a white shirt and red trousers which only went down as far as his soft, floppy brown-leather boots. Mum said he was a Cavalier and Dad said he wasn't. Both of them seemed to have become historians for the day.

Standing by the biggest four-poster bed Poppy had ever seen, the Cavalier or the not-Cavalier told them how King Charles I was imprisoned at Hampton Court until he escaped when his guards were looking the other way. In an overloud whisper to Mum, Dad made a comparison with his own departure, a joke which Mum did not find exactly funny. Then Dad said that he should not be cavalier with his comparisons and she *did* find that funny though Poppy knew that no one else would, ever. One of their group, a tall woman with reddish-brown hair, beautifully manicured hands, a yellow cashmere jersey and a slight stoop, asked the man a question about Henry VIII. When he answered, Dad flinched slightly as if the answer hurt him and he whispered to Poppy, 'That's not quite right, actually.'

Poppy blushed and hissed, 'Don't you dare say anything,'

and Mum heard that and raised her eyebrows to signal that she agreed and that seemed to do the trick as he kept his big mouth shut.

***

They were walking through the rose garden, along a gravel path that crunched under their feet, when the sky darkened and the first drops of rain fell. Lara watched as the leaves began to shine and water dripped down the stems. These flowerbeds seemed to have been forgotten: clumps of weeds were growing between the bushes and piles of shrivelled roses lay uncollected in corners.

They joined the queue for the maze. In front of them was a silent family of three: he was tall and thin with short blond hair, and she was short and plump and pushing a three-wheeled buggy containing a sleeping child. Each of them, Lara felt, was in a world of their own. Jamie showed their tickets to the woman at the gate and stepped inside as the rain made the hedges crackle, and tiny pools of water appeared on the asphalt path.

'Poppy and I will race you to the middle,' said Lara.

'No, it will be more fun together,' said Jamie.

She shook her head. 'You've read up on the maze, I'm sure you know the way. Give us two minutes.'

'Why? Why do you always do this?' he asked, not caring too much that Poppy was listening.

'Do what?'

'Go off,' he said, though he meant *Go off with Poppy.*

'Jamie, this is a game.'

'Please, please shut up both of you,' said Poppy. 'Dad and I will go together. Three minutes. Ok?'

'Ok.'

'Ok'

Lara shut her eyes for a moment, not because it was part of the game but because she was cross with herself for quarrelling with Jamie in front of Poppy. On opening them, she followed the hedge on her left even though at times she could see that it was leading nowhere. She began to miss turnings, she walked without a plan, without knowing where she was going. She overtook a young American couple arguing about which way to go and she herself was passed by two teenage boys who seemed to be screaming for the sake of screaming. The low grey cloud overhead made the maze seem so dark that at times she had the sense that she had been walking all afternoon and that dusk was approaching. As she walked, she could hear the hum of traffic in the distance, the cries of peacocks, and the squawks of the parakeets. Then she heard Jamie's voice on the other side of the hedge, but that soon disappeared.

A moment later she thought she heard Jamie again but now his voice had changed. He was laughing, though something told her that he wasn't laughing with Poppy, he had either met someone else or he was using his iPhone when really he should be looking after his daughter. She tried to listen, without admitting to herself that she was trying to listen. She walked on until she could no longer hear him.

But then she turned a corner and found the middle of the maze where there were two benches and a couple of trees. Poppy was bending over her iPhone and Jamie was talking on his iPhone with a smile on his face which she had never seen before. Over the years, more than one person had told her what a lovely smile Jamie had. The comment would make her think of all his different smiles. The smile when he understood a joke, the smile when Poppy came home from school, the smile when the car started on a cold morning, the smile when he remembered that she didn't have to get up early. But though she had never seen *this* smile before, she understood at once that he was speaking to a woman and she also understood that he really *really* liked this woman.

***

'You remember looking near here?' asked Lara, as the funny round church appeared on their right.

'Moving is so stressful, I'm glad we stayed put,' he said, forgetfully.

Lara looked out of the window and wondered, as she often wondered, how things would have turned out if they had moved house. She thought about what they hadn't done because everything else seemed connected. What they hadn't done was untainted, it hadn't failed, in a world somewhere it was happening. A different house, a different school, a different social life, different conversations leading to different thoughts, different thoughts leading to different actions, different actions leading to different consequences. Nothing would have been the same. She knew of course that things could have turned out worse than they had but she couldn't really believe it.

Jamie was speeding up. He was going to the Law Centre that evening and he couldn't be late for that.

'How's Anaïs?' she asked.

'Her neighbours are vile.'

'You're going to help?'

'Yes, but … I might not be the best person.'

'I'm sure you are. She's very lucky to have you.'

'As you know, I want to go to Glasgow for a week over Christmas, so Anaïs might be better off finding someone else.'

Lara glanced in the mirror and saw that Poppy was wearing her headphones whilst she read. 'We need,' she said, 'to speak about Christmas.'

'We do. As you know, I want to take Poppy with me,' he said casually, as if he was talking about a trip to the shops. 'She hasn't seen her cousins for ages.' Lara found herself remembering the advice she'd received last year. If you think that you might lose your temper/open another bottle/buy a packet of cigarettes etc., begin to count. She'd received a lot of advice last year. … One, two, three. 'If she wants to go to Glasgow,' she said, 'then you can take her at half-term.'

'But the boys are expecting her.'

One. She couldn't believe what she was hearing. 'Then you shouldn't have told them!'

'She doesn't have any brothers and sisters,' said Jamie, pausing a moment, doubtless in case she'd forgotten that fact and needed time to take it on board, 'and that makes her cousins all the more important.'

One, two. 'I know she doesn't have any brothers and sisters, Jamie.'

'In any case,' he said, 'you usually have to work over Christmas, so I thought it might be good for you not to have Poppy to worry about. And you know that Phillip hasn't been well, he'd really like to see her.'

There we are, she thought, a classic example of a Jamie move: he justifies what he wants to do by appealing to altruism.

'So this,' she asked, 'is my Christmas present, is it?'

He turned towards her. 'What is it with you and arguments, Lara? Why do you have to argue about every damn thing? You are impossible.'

'Keep your eyes on the road, Jamie,' she said as her right foot pressed an imaginary brake pedal.

She started to count again and this time she didn't stop when she reached five. She wanted to stop but she didn't dare, not because she'd say something she'd regret but because she was worried that she might cry and she didn't want him of all people to see her cry … ten, eleven …. She could just about handle not having any work and, if she tried really hard, she thought she could cope with the possibility of a long drawn-out row about Poppy living with him for half the week. But to spend Christmas alone? She'd actually been looking forward to Christmas this year, not because she had any reason to do so but because it was, well, Christmas, and it seemed to promise a break from a world where there had to a reason for everything. There would be zero chance of the court listing an application before then, and in any case, she was the one who said that Poppy would never forgive them for litigating. … Fifteen, sixteen … At a push, Poppy might understand litigation about where she was going to live but not about a few days over Christmas. She was too much a child to understand such childishness. Which meant that they would have a big row and he would win. Jamie would never give in. That was part of his job. He was a litigator. *Litigare* to argue. No wonder they got on so well. No wonder they got on so badly. His brother had been ill and doubtless he would like to see Jamie and Poppy, but there had been a number of times when Phillip had come down to London for one of his Wordsworth conferences and had not seen them … twenty-one, twenty-two … She had spent one Christmas alone, in a studio flat in Dalston, the year before she met Jamie, and afterwards she swore to herself that she would never do so again. She knew that what makes spending Christmas alone so awful is that you are never alone. She didn't know how much she believed in the truth of Christmas but she knew that every year she seemed to accumulate within herself memories of Christmas, memories which began with images of snow and troikas and the sound of bells, all of which she may or may not have experienced, and the smell of tangerines and nutmeg and candles together with the sense of absolutely safety, all of which she certainly had experienced … twenty-seven, twenty-eight … As Lara counted, she felt for a moment she was counting Christmases of the past, Christmases which she could never have believed she would one day look back on and think that they were less than perfect though they must have contained within themselves the seeds of the conflicts which were later revealed … Christmases which were leading to the Christmases of the future … thirty, thirty one … where Jamie was speeding through empty Glaswegian streets with Poppy in the front seat whilst she stayed at home counting out her life in Christmases … but now the numbers began to jump around and when they began to seem more real than the Christmases she was remembering, she suddenly understood that she was reading a telephone number on the back of a Polish lorry and that they were so close to that lorry that she felt she could reach out and touch the numbers. Later, much later, she would remember how for a split second she had confusedly thought that what was really important was that she should stick out her arm to stop Poppy and Jamie going through the windscreen. The car slowed down.

'Jesus, Jamie,' she said as her scalp prickled.

'Sorry about that, people,' said Jamie, casual as ever.

'What happened?' asked Poppy.

'We nearly had an accident,' said Lara.

'Ok,' said Poppy. 'This book's fantastic.'

9th December

To: Larissa@ChatsworthChambers.com
From: Pentecost@ChatsworthChambers.com

Maguire – boundary dispute

Mr Evelyn called about the Advice. He wants it by lunchtime as he's going skiing tomorrow.

Regards
Pentecost Burnett

Practice Manager

10th December

To: Pentecost@ChatsworthChambers.com
From: Larissa@ChatsworthChambers.com

Maguire – boundary dispute

When I sent in the Advice yesterday, Mr Evelyn called me. He wasn't happy that I said that his client would lose. I explained that he would lose because he doesn't own the land on which he has built his summerhouse. When he said that I was speculating, I asked him if he had read the Land Registry office copies which he sent me. He made me wait whilst he found them and read them. He wasn't very happy. In fact I couldn't help hearing him shouting at someone in the office. He said that he would call you. I think that means that he wants to renegotiate my brief fee. Please stick to what was agreed.

Regards
Lara

11th December

AT LUNCHTIME, ARCHIE WENT to Caffè Nero on Clapham High Street and sat at a table in the window where he ate a toasted mozzarella sandwich and drank a bottle of tomato juice. Like almost everyone else in the café, including the staff, he passed the time looking at his phone. He hadn't heard from Lara since the WhatsApp message she had sent him yesterday while on the way to Hampton Court with her ex. He had tried to call her in the evening but without success. He knew that he shouldn't be worrying but that didn't stop him worrying. It was part of the magic of their new friendship that the two of them were constantly in touch, and there on his iPhone was the evidence: masses of inconsequential texts. In a way, the more inconsequential they were, the better.

'Sorry I'm late, Archie, really sorry.' Archie looked up to see a smiling Benedict holding a mug of hot chocolate and a pain au raisin. That smile. Meg was right about Benedict being good-looking. He had brown curly hair on the longish side and a suntan which never seemed to fade. But his eyes were large and sad.

'I had a call from Harry,' he was saying. 'He helps me run the Old Boy's Hockey team.'

Archie knew nothing about hockey save that people chased a ball around with sticks. 'Season's going well?'

Benedict shook his head. 'Not really, Archie. In fact since lockdown it's become a bit of a nightmare. People just don't want to give up their Saturday afternoons, I spend half my life on the phone and the other half sending emails. Most of the time, I'm just ignored.'

'It must be very frustrating,' said his employer.

When Archie managed to turn the discussion to the sale of the Clapham Park flat, he was relieved to hear that Benedict had it all in hand. The tenant, he said, was entitled to stay for a further eighteen months but he was sure that she would leave any day now. From the sound of it, the two of them had struck up a good relationship, with Benedict calling her almost every day. They hadn't actually agreed on the sweetener, but Benedict thought that it would be about £1,000. Archie could live with that.

'I'll go and talk to her and find out what she'll accept,' drawled Benedict with that confidence that nothing could go wrong which, against his better judgement, Archie found himself admiring.

'Do be careful. If you try and force her out, we could end up with criminal records.'

Benedict smiled reassuringly. 'Don't you worry, Archie, you won't end up in prison.'

'I'm glad to hear it.'

Benedict thought for a moment. 'One of the monks at school used to visit prisoners. Dom Anselm. I think I've mentioned him before.'

'I think you have, Benedict.' Like about twenty times.

Archie had noticed before that when he spoke to Benedict, his voice would change slightly. It would sound almost upper-class or at least more like the upper-class characters he and Meg watched on television. Was he trying to make Benedict feel at home?

'Let me know how you get on. But don't worry, you'll be fine, Benedict. When you're with her, just try and relax.'

'Will do, Archie, will do.'

12th December

To: Larissa@ChatsworthChambers.com
From: Pentecost@ChatsworthChambers.com

Maguire – boundary dispute

You were right. Mr Evelyn did call. He asked if I knew anyone who might want to buy a summerhouse. I think that was a joke but with solicitors you can never really tell. He said that it wasn't fair on his client to have to pay the agreed fee given that you did not provide the answer. I told him that the fee had been agreed and that it was not conditional in any sense. He became quite cross. He said that if you did not play ball he would pull all work from Chambers.

Regards
Pentecost Burnett

Practice Manager

13th December

'DO WE REALLY WANT a Christmas story next time?' asked Georgie, getting up from the sofa and knocking into the Christmas tree which Poppy had decorated that afternoon. She reached for the bottle of the excellent white burgundy which Giles had supplied. 'Oops, sorry,' she added as a silver bauble fell off and broke.

'Yes, I think that we do,' said Lara. 'Let's put Christmas off for another month.'

'Definitely,' said Amanda. 'Something light. I thought that this one would never end, it was like a bad trip, it was worse than Henry James. The little boy took twenty pages to get out of bed.'

'What a brat,' said Georgie, as she topped up her glass. 'If I'd have been his mother, I'd have given him a clip round the ear.'

Lara glanced at her watch and wondered how long they would stay. Three of the usual crowd were absent – problems with children, problems with partners, problems with work – which hadn't made things easier. She felt that she herself had blathered on enough. As she was hosting the meeting, she had had to introduce the work and speak for ten minutes about the author. That was the deal. It had gone quite well. At least Amanda had kept awake and Georgie hadn't made her usual unfunny joke about Lara only reading Tolstoy. Not that Lara had any illusions about having a profound understanding, perhaps any understanding, of what was after all a notoriously difficult work. But she had done her best. She had prepped the book as she prepped her briefs. The same instruments were apparent – the blue counsel's notebook, the yellow Post-it notes, the red and black half-chewed pencil – and the same determination to ignore all distractions.

She hadn't just read what Jamie liked to call the text, she'd been into the attic to look through his books where she had found a short life of the author by an American writer and a collection of essays by Martha Nussbaum, one of which she'd read without, it is true, understanding what on earth she was on about. But Lara felt that this non-legal work was a step in the right direction. Finding or rather making time seemed right. It wasn't just Jamie who had put work before everything, she'd been just as bad. Hadn't she put her practice before everything other than Poppy for the last fifteen years? In fact, could she put her hand on her heart and say that she had never put work before Poppy?

'Robert and I always argued at Christmas,' Amanda was saying. 'Sometimes we even argued about arguing at Christmas.' Lara was surprised and pleased by what Amanda said. It was the first time she'd heard her speak about Robert since he'd died in a less than wholly positive way. Nor was she wearing the bandana and nor was she smoking her roll-ups.

'I'm beginning to think that we worry too much about arguments,' said Georgie, sipping her glass of wine. 'Couples argue, they always have and they always will. I expect that arguments perform a biological function. They show the offspring how to conduct themselves without using violence, which must be good for the tribe. In any case, I can't see that they can do any harm. After all, they're only words.'

'Words, yes,' said Amanda, 'but they are also lines on the face and ulcers.'

'And strokes and heart attacks,' said Georgie. 'Your go Lara.'

'Don't be stupid, Georgie. Actually, I think that arguments at least show that you care,' said Lara.

'But what were you doing in the car with him?' asked Georgie, reacting ninety minutes late to Lara's account of their near miss on the A3. From the way Georgie spoke, Lara thought, you'd believe Lara and Poppy had gone for a drive with a notorious axe murderer.

'I didn't tell you?' she replied, hoping that her irritation wouldn't show. 'We were coming back from Hampton Court. The Palace.'

'Why did you agree to go?' asked Georgie as if she was astonished.

She wasn't of course. Like so many successful members of the bar, she was very much the actor manqué. Lara let her wait for a moment before answering in the flattest tone she could find this side of rudeness. 'I've known him for fifteen years and he happens to be Poppy's father.'

'I think we should get back to what we were discussing before,' said lovely Amanda.

For a while they tried, but for Lara at least it was all becoming a little tiring. The periods of silence were lengthening and the evening's conversation was becoming a series of isolated and unrelated comments, not all of them about what they had been reading. A promising three-way dialogue on the theme of time somehow turned into a discussion of where to buy Christmas decorations. After that, Amanda had read out in her lovely smoky voice an amazing stop-you-in-your-tracks passage where her favourite character says that he had wasted years of his life, had experienced his greatest love, had longed to die, and all for a woman whom he now realised did not appeal to him and was not even his type. When Amanda had finished, there was a kind of holy silence for half a minute. But after that, and Lara never really worked out how it happened, there was a discussion about what you do if you buy the wrong size turkey, whether you can take it back, whether you should freeze it or whether to make do. Georgie was for freezing and Amanda was for making do, though she complicated matters by wondering if she should become a vegetarian and even asked Lara if the author under discussion had been a vegetarian, Lara now apparently being the expert on the back of having read the book by the American. Surely, Lara thought, it was time to wind up.

For a while they returned to the topic of obsessive love and where on earth could they find it. But the subject must have been exhausted because Georgie began again. 'Amanda, you heard that he wants to take the wee girl for half the week?'

'So Lara said,' answered Amanda, giving Lara a smile which advised patience and yet somehow managed to express a shared frustration.

'Lara, you know what I think we should do?' said Georgie, dropping her copy of the book on the floor as if she wanted to signal that the literary part of the evening was over. 'We should file an application for a Child Arrangement Order before he does. There's no reason to hang around and wait for him to do it. Let's take him by surprise.' She sounded for all the world like a child playing pirates.

'I'll think about it,' said Lara, wondering if she could take away their glasses without appearing rude.

'Don't you think that Lara and Jamie should try and work something out?' asked Amanda, glancing at Lara. 'It's not complicated, there's just him and her, there's no one else involved.'

'What do you mean by that?' asked Georgie.

'Just that if they had partners who had their own children, the arrangements would be more difficult.'

'But how do you know there's no one else involved?' said Lara. 'Every time I see him, he's wearing something new. Someone's taking him shopping, he would never go by himself.'

'Don't be ridiculous, Lara,' said Georgie.

'Yes, don't be ridiculous, Lara.'

'How do you know there's no one else?'

Amanda sighed, as if she was dealing with someone more than usually obtuse. 'Because he told me, last week. I saw him at Clapham Common station, we had a chat whilst we were waiting for the train. What's more …'

'What do you mean, "What's more …?"' Lara asked.

Amanda didn't answer immediately. She stared at Georgie for a moment and then turned to Lara. 'What's more, there never was anyone else,' she said quietly.

'He said that?' asked Lara.

'Yes. I've known him for almost as long as you have, Lara.'

'Doesn't mean that he's telling the truth.'

'I meant that's why I was talking to him.'

'You don't have to justify that,' said Lara, wanting to get away from them, not knowing what to say, not quite believing what she had heard but also feeling in the pit of her stomach the sense of dread which reminded her of how she felt when she thought that she might have made a terrible mistake at work. 'I'm just going to check that Poppy's ok,' she said, standing up and quickly leaving the room.

Poppy was sitting up in bed in white and red flannel pyjamas reading *Tender is the Night.* Lara sat down beside her and hugged her and not once did Poppy take her eyes off the page.

'Everything ok, darling?' asked Lara.

Poppy continued reading but managed to look puzzled as she did so. 'Yes. Why shouldn't it be?' she said with her eyes moving across the page.

'No reason,' said Lara.

Poppy now looked up. 'They like the tree?'

'They love it, darling.'

She laid the book down and looked up at Lara. There was a little toothpaste on the side of her mouth. 'Actually, Mum, things are not that ok.'

'You mean at school?'

'Yes. It's still going on.'

'The stupid Putin jokes?'

'Yes. Some of them won't talk to me.'

'It's prejudice, darling. People get ideas into their heads and won't let go.'

'Makes me cross. Anyway, as I'm as much Scottish as I am Russian. They know nothing about the war. They probably couldn't find Russia on a map.'

'Of course they know nothing. Do you want me to speak to Mrs Mitchell?'

'No, I think that would make it worse.'

'But you're getting on well with Jess?'

'Yes, and you're getting on well with Dad?'

'Yes, I think I am.'

Halfway down the stairs she heard Georgie holding forth about an application under the Children Act and her heart sank. For Georgie, the idea of making such an application could not have been more straightforward but for Lara it felt like a huge hill to climb. A few years ago, she herself would have taken it in her stride. She'd been a feisty pupil, a feisty young member of chambers, but she no longer felt feisty. She felt feistied out. Now an application felt like an act of despair. To offer up your child for the decision of a busy and bored district judge? Didn't she and Jamie have a duty to decide how to look after their child? And did not that duty include having to argue with each other where necessary? Georgie, she knew, wouldn't understand her reluctance; she'd make the perfectly obvious point that Lara and Jamie would only be asking the court to decide if they could not agree between themselves. She'd also say that Lara herself had acted in dozens of such cases without ever questioning the sense of what she was doing. She'd say that Lara knew the law, that Lara knew her rights, that Lara knew what to do. But that wasn't true. She didn't know what to do and she was beginning to think that this was not a case of not knowing the right answer but a case of there not being a right answer.

Nor were her doubts just about Poppy and Jamie. Yesterday, during a conference in chambers about a property dispute, she had found herself giving advice while all the time thinking that she might just as well have been saying the opposite. Why should Mrs Jones be given the house and not Mr Jones? Or why should Mr Jones be given the pension and not Mrs Jones? She didn't understand why she was doubting. She knew that it wasn't because she had just remembered a case which had blown her conclusion out of the water. This was not about fallibility, nor was it because she was feeling perverse. Afterwards, she felt almost dishonest: she'd accepted the brief fee but hadn't told them what she believed.

By the time that Lara came back into the room, Georgie had moved onto the question of which counsel Jamie would choose. 'You know he'll probably instruct silk?' she said as Lara sat down. The second bottle was half empty, and two wooden camels, a wooden Father Christmas and two plastic reindeer lay on the floor under the tree.

'You're kidding?' said Lara, looking at the clock on the wall for a longer period than she needed for purely informational purposes.

'He was always talking about his silks, wasn't he?' said Georgie, nodding as if she was agreeing with herself. 'One of them will want to do him a favour. That's how it works,' she added for Amanda's benefit. 'He won't stand a chance, though it should be interesting.'

Interesting? Lara had a pretty good idea what Georgie meant by 'interesting' and it wasn't 'legally interesting.' 'Interesting' here meant seeing whether she could make Jamie lose his rag in court. Lara liked Georgie but she couldn't help thinking that a torturer might use the expression 'should be interesting' in a similar way.

'Lara,' said Georgie, 'don't look so glum. Everything will be fine.'

'I don't want to make an application and I don't know what I should be doing. It's hard to admit that, but it's true. And I don't know what the court would say. That would partly depend on which judge you get. What a nightmare.'

'A bigger nightmare,' said Georgie would be Jamie having the wee girl live with him whilst he is shacked up with some floozie.'

Then the doorbell rang, which Lara subsequently thought possibly saved her friendship with Georgie. 'That will be Giles,' said Georgie, standing up and looking at her watch. 'The bugger's on time for once.'

But it wasn't Giles, it was Jamie and a woman of about 25 who was very beautiful and a little drunk. 'Good evening,' she said, putting her hand on the door frame. She had jet-black hair, cut in a fringe which put Lara in mind of Cleopatra, and a tiny gold stud on the side of her nose.

Jamie leaned forward. He was drunk too, drunker if anything. 'This is Anaïs. You know, she teaches Giles's and Georgie's children French. I mean she teaches Cordelia and Carmel ....'

Anaïs giggled senselessly. 'Jamie's been advising me,' she said with a strong French accent.

'Not sure how well,' he said, giggling too, as if Anaïs had moved on from teaching French to teaching giggling.

Lara could tell he was drunk because as well as the usual signs, he wasn't wearing a coat, just a new grey suit with the blue check shirt she'd bought him for his birthday three years ago. His hair had been cut since she last saw him; in fact she'd never seen it so short. When they were together, his hair had been long and wavy. What she also noticed were his ears. For a moment she didn't know what to say because she was wondering how she could have lived with Jamie for so long and not noticed that his ears were a tiny bit too large. If she hadn't noticed that, then what else hadn't she noticed?

'Can we come in?'

When he said that, she became aware that the conversation in the kitchen had stopped. 'Not sure if that's a good idea,' she said, as she retreated and closed the kitchen door. 'We've a book-club meeting.'

'Oh, yes,' he said. 'Last Thursday of the month.'

She could smell the alcohol on his breath. 'It's Tuesday.'

He put his hand on the door frame. 'Last Tuesday ...'

'But it's usually on a Wednesday.'

'Is that Daddy?' Poppy was calling from the top of the stairs.

Jamie took a step towards her and almost slipped before Anaïs steadied him. 'Hullo, Poppy, I've just come to drop something off.' He was holding, Lara now saw, a large brown envelope marked with her name in black marker.

Lara turned round. 'Go back to bed, darling, Daddy's just going.' She watched Poppy disappear.

'Instructions,' he said, offering her the envelope. 'Day after tomorrow. Bromley County Court. It used to be your favourite. Kent's own *Palais de Justice*, the missing paragraph from Pevsner…'

'Instructions? You're joking. I can't act for your firm.'

He ignored her. 'You'll love it. I'll call Pentecost in the morning.'

'What if something goes wrong?'

He laughed. 'You could do it standing on your head.'

There was something else odd. 'Why are you *delivering* it? What's wrong with email?'

But his mind was elsewhere. 'Lara,' he whispered, his mood dropping like a stone, 'I can't go to Scotland. They want me to work between Christmas and the New Year.' He was referring to the partners at his firm.

She asked herself what Poppy would say. 'Ok, Jamie, good night,' she said, sensing Georgie behind her as she closed the door. 'He wasn't wearing a coat. But why did he come round?' She showed Georgie the envelope. 'Instructions. Why didn't he email them or put them in the DX?'

'He was always a boozer,' replied Georgie, as if that answered the question.

'Did you know that he was out with Anaïs?'

For a fraction of a second Georgie seemed embarrassed. 'Her neighbours have been harassing her so I put her in touch with the Advice Centre. I suppose that's where Jamie met her.'

14th December

BENEDICT WAS SITTING IN his Land Rover outside Archie's Clapham Park flat when he heard the whine of a milk van. That peculiar sound so redolent of other mornings brought him to his senses. He had been dozing off with the heater on full blast, Handel's *Messiah* in the CD player and a stick of incense smouldering in the ashtray. For a moment he had the delicious sense that he was back in chapel, snug with his friends on each side and a packet of Opal Fruits in his pocket. Not that he was wild about *Messiah*: too many references to sheep for his liking, you'd think that it had been written for Border Collies. But Ma always played *Messiah* at Christmas.

Benedict watched as a mangey dog fox trotted up to the yellow skip thirty feet away. Compared to Somerset foxes it was just skin and bone. It seemed to think about jumping up but instead slinked off. The skip was overflowing with plasterboards and floorboards, kitchen cupboards, tiles, metal pipes, an old lavatory, and a two-legged stool. He'd passed other skips along the road. In London everyone was doing up their houses and flats, everyone was buying or selling, no one was standing still, everyone was moving.

He looked up at the first-floor window of the converted Victorian villa and saw that the curtains remained closed. He told himself that when they opened, he would go and speak to Ms Saint Ledger the tenant. He hadn't actually met her yet though he'd called her a number of times without of course saying who he was. Time to move on, he would say, time to move on. Occasionally, he would put on silly voices, former schoolmasters usually, impressions which had always gone down well with friends in the past. After a while, she'd blocked his calls. He'd also sent her a number of postcards with the same message, one or two had pictures of the late Queen and a couple were of the Household Cavalry.

Now his phone was ringing. It was Archie. Why was he calling so early?

'Good morning, Archie.'

'Any news?' Archie was nervous, that was obvious.

'Not yet, Archie. I'm going to meet her today, don't you worry,' he said as a blackbird sang in one of the neighbouring gardens.

Archie waited a moment before replying. 'You'll be careful, won't you? You know what to say? You don't think that I should come with you?'

'It will be fine,' he said, knowing that Archie would not be reassured whatever he said.

'Alright. Speak later.'

Benedict put his phone back in the pocket of his Barbour. He was beginning to find Archie irritating. He was stuck in the past. He went on and on about bloody Brexit. God, that was boring. And why did Megan have to leave? They had got on so well at his interview. She didn't press him too hard about his qualifications, she seemed to guess that he'd never finished any course he'd started. He'd told her that his parents had tenants on the estate, he'd gown up with that experience. Either you know how to manage tenants or you don't. After they gave him the job, she stayed around for a few weeks to show him the ropes. She was so efficient, she had files for every property, files for repairs, for gas safety, for fire, for Council Tax, files for everything under the sun. That was the way to run a business, he thought, you have files. On the passenger seat beside him was the file for this flat. He would wave that around this morning. He wasn't sure what to say to the tenant but knew that he would think of something when the time came. He always did. After that he would take off for Somerset and give Ma a nice surprise.

15th December

To: JamieAubrie@lawmail.com
From: Larissa@ChatsworthChambers.com

I've been given a couple of tickets for *Don Giovanni* at the Coliseum on Tuesday night. Are you free? It starts at 7pm.

Regards
Lara

16th December

To: Larissa@ChatsworthChambers.com
From: JamieAubrie@lawmail.com

Hi Lara
Thanks but I have a trial on Wednesday and I need to prepare a trial bundle. I'll end up working late. I hope that you enjoy it.

With best wishes
Jamie

17th December

'THEY IGNORE HER, THEY'VE been ignoring her for three years now, that's why she works at home so much. You would have thought that she invaded Ukraine.'

'I think that you're a little too fond of her, Pentecost. Should I be jealous?'

'No, no, this is serious. When she walks into the library, the talking stops.'

'Has she ever spoken about the war?'

'Once, she was in tears, Lucy. She has relatives in Odesa and in Moscow. Her view is the same as ours.'

'I remember you saying that she was unhappy.'

'It doesn't matter what you believe, it matters who you are.'

'I know.'

'I hear things, they talk about her, they talk as if I'm not there.'

'Might be on account of your colour, Pentecost.'

'Might be on account of them thinking themselves such superior beings.'

'Perhaps it's time for you to retire? How old are you?'

'You know how old I am.'

'I could retire, too. We could spend our winters in Italy.'

'We could, Lucia, we could.'

'She is very beautiful.'

'How do you know? You looked on our website?'

'No, she was before me last year. A boundary dispute.'

'You never mentioned that.'

'I can't remember anything about the case. I just remember her eyes. So lovely but so sad.'

18th December

LARA WALKED ALONG THE side of the Common towards Clapham Common station through what was almost a snowstorm. She was wearing her black bobble hat, her Max Mara coat and a grey Brora scarf which Jamie had bought her for Christmas two years before. She caught sight of her reflection in a hairdresser's window: she looked like some strange creature who had come out of the darkness. And that in fact is how she felt. No one had wanted to come to the opera with her. Everyone was doing something with somebody else. She found herself remembering those times over the last three years when she had walked into a room and the conversation had stopped. *Come on Lara,* she told herself, as she walked down the steps into the station, *less of the self-pity, please. It will probably do you good to spend an evening alone.*

When the train arrived, she found a seat without too much difficulty. The floor was wet with traces of melted snow. Next to her was a woman with black leggings and a white T-shirt under a black coat. For a moment Lara wondered if the woman was pregnant. On her other side was an elderly man wearing a black homburg, a herringbone coat and highly polished black shoes. She idly wondered if she would be able to see her reflection in them. A family of three sat opposite her. The parents were about her and Jamie's ages, the little girl was about 12, two years younger than Poppy. She wasn't surprised to see a family of three opposite her, since the break-up, she'd seen families of three everywhere she'd looked. She sometimes thought that she was followed by families of three. Not all of them looked deliriously happy but all of them seemed conscious that whatever difficulties the day might hold they were at least together.

She found herself remembering the last time she and Jamie went to the opera. It was the one about the fox, she couldn't remember what it was called, and as evenings out go, it wasn't one of the best. All had begun well. They had walked over the Common together on a hot September afternoon when the trees were still in leaf, and dogs were being walked, and children were playing football. They'd had a glass of Prosecco before it began, and then another during the interval. Perhaps that was one too many. Soon after the third act began, she'd whispered a question about the plot and Jamie had put on the face his mother would use if you tried to talk to her in church. There was a definite sense with Jamie that he was more musical than thou.

On the Tube on the way home she had been silly enough to refer to certain children's films with talking animals, which made him cross or pretend-cross, she wasn't quite sure which. Either way, she ended up having to listen to a lecture. You have to work at it, he said as the doors opened at Charing Cross. Comprehension is as essential to the enjoyment of opera as it is to Shakespeare, you can't just let it wash over you. That, he said, as if he was lecturing a classroom of not very bright students, is a temptation which has to be resisted. When the train was pulling out of Embankment he was making a point about music and representation. At Kennington he referred to the views of Theodore Adorno. Was it her imagination or did the West Indian woman standing by the door wink at her? At Oval he began to let her – and anyone else in the carriage who was listening – know about Wagner's writings on the subject, something about having the lights on in the opera house so that people could read the score. Adorno disappeared at Stockwell but Thomas Mann was with them all the way to Clapham Common. Coming out of the station and feeling the first touch of autumn in the air she had begun to push back. She pointed out that Jamie did not read music. Did that mean that he understood and enjoyed music less than someone who did? What would he have done in Bayreuth? He himself had once told her that Luciano Pavarotti did not read music. But did that mean that Pavarotti did not understand and enjoy music? Of course not. Even she could see that he was a great musician. Wasn't there a danger, she said, of being too analytic, too intellectual? After a silence which sounded as brooding as any in Tchaikovsky, he asked her what she was trying to say. She said that perhaps he took opera just a little too seriously? As they turned into their road, he said that it was obvious that she didn't really enjoy opera and she said, in that snappy way she sometimes had, 'Do you know what, Jamie, I think you're right.' What she didn't explain was that she had gone to the opera to be with him. But they never went to the opera together again.

***

In the foyer she felt more alone than ever and possibly less excited than anyone else in the building. The hubbub was deafening. For a moment she even thought about going home – never had the prospect of half a bottle of wine seemed more enticing. On the ceiling was a goddess peering down on everyone with an expression which suggested that she was trying to understand what all the fuss was about. The red carpet and the gilded walls added to Lara's sense that it was all rather silly. She thought that people were looking at her, especially the few who were by themselves. They were pretending to read their programmes, but she wasn't fooled. She saw a man with snow on his shoulders carrying a book which they had discussed in their recent book-club meeting. That was rather spooky, and for a mad moment she wondered if she should go and talk to him. But then his wife or partner or girlfriend came up to him and handed him a programme. She couldn't help noticing that nearly everyone else was older than her, not as old as the Wigmore Hall crowd but pretty ancient, nonetheless. She watched a woman with a fur stole on her shoulders and lines on her forehead like a musical score hug a man with a port-coloured face who could not have been less than 90. Three stooping men, all immaculately dressed, shrieked with laughter at something a fourth had said.

She resisted the allure of the bar and found her seat near the front of the dress circle without too much trouble. It was generally where Jamie used to sit, and, looking around, she half expected to see him. Perhaps he would be on a date with one of those trainees he used to mention a little too often. A man standing at the end of her row caught her eye and she stood up to let him pass. In fact, his ticket was for the seat next to Lara's and he wasted no time in introducing himself. He was called Michael and the first thing he said was that he'd never been to the opera before. 'I think I will find it difficult,' he said, with mock seriousness. 'I am not very musical.' He told her how at 30 he had tried to learn the violin and that his teacher had despaired of him, how the teacher's cat had walked out of lessons as soon as he started playing. Lara found herself laughing. He had a nice line in self-deprecation. Her age. Divorced. One child. Pensions adviser. Walton-on-Thames. The way in which he neatly summarised his life made Lara think that he was not unused to internet dating. He was chatty, which was nice, not that she was looking for company but it was a bit of a strain being quiet when everyone else was talking. He began to ask her about *Don Giovanni*, and for once she was the one who was able to answer the questions or at least make a good stab at doing so.

When the curtain rose, Lara saw that the action was set in eighteenth-century Italy, which would have appealed to Jamie who had a somewhat conservative attitude towards radical productions. For years he had blamed the Royal Opera House for killing his mother, who had a stroke after having to sit through the infamous nuclear-submarine production of *The Flying Dutchman*. He had been a child at the time but he would always remember the horror of finding the red programme lying on the kitchen floor the following morning.

This evening's nod towards realism did not however stop the producer introducing a witchcraft theme – Donna Anna was wearing a pointy hat – which made little sense to Lara. In fact, she found herself getting irritated with the director. Even she could see the absurdity of it. Jamie used to say that you can't understand a lot of modern productions until you realise that the people making them hate opera. Beside her, Michael was trying, albeit *sotto voce*, to continue their conversation. She put her finger to her lips and smiled.

***

Lara looked at her watch and saw that there was still half an hour to the interval. She had read up on the opera that afternoon, which in the circumstances hadn't helped as much as it should it have done. She tried to look at her watch but as she strained her eyes she heard an aria which she remembered having heard before. Her first reaction was to question how anything could be quite so beautiful as Zerlina's plea to be forgiven, made to her rather goonish boyfriend who was standing stock-still in his too-tight leather jerkin. The conductor was leaning so far forward that it looked as if he might topple over, a woman next to her was looking at her phone and beside her on the other side Michael was quietly sleeping. But as the aria floated across the auditorium, nothing else seemed of the slightest importance, nothing seemed worth worrying about. As Lara listened, she seemed to understand that everything she had ever read about Mozart counted for absolutely nothing. Even thinking about the music was beside the point. When it seemed to be over, she felt that she couldn't try and make sense of it, all she could do was to remember it. It was complete in itself, it was as complete as a triangle. And yet she was aware that she'd heard the aria before. She was sure that she had never seen this opera but she remembered a CD of arias which Jamie would play over and over whilst they decorated their flat in Hackney. Leon something. Price? Leontyne Price, that was it. And then, just as Lara thought that the aria was over, it began again and this time she saw not just the flat and its green and white paint but their world at that time, all that they knew, all that they loved. What was so odd, so odd that it made her feel quite dizzy, was that that world seemed to contain not only the persons and objects of their daily life and not only the weather of that day a year ago. It contained everything including all their hopes for the future, hopes which were just as much a part of their world as each other. That world, their world, now felt more real to her than her world today, a world of anger and emails. Soon, too soon, she sensed that the music was coming to an end. She so wanted it to continue, she felt it had to continue, and yet as it ended, she saw that it had to end, that that made it complete in a way in which nothing else was complete. When it drew to a close there was a delicious moment of silence, and for the first time that evening she felt absolutely at one with everyone else in the auditorium. After people started clapping, she found herself looking up at the surtitles with eyes full of tears.

19th December

VERONICA, THE HOUSING OFFICER whom Lara was supposed to be meeting at court, was late, and so Lara sat down on one of the uncomfortable seats in the waiting area and reread Jamie's brief. He had been right to say it was straightforward: the client, St Patrick's Housing Association, wanted to evict a tenant who had rent arrears of £8,000, and that was all there was to it. Or so she thought. She put the brief back in her bag and looked around. The place was crowded as it always was on a Thursday morning when, for reasons best known to itself, the court listed a number of hearings at 10.30 am. People were chatting or reading newspapers or staring into space. Sitting next to their clients, or leaning over them, were the lawyers, the solicitors with their files, the barristers with their briefs. In the far corner, a group stood out from the rest. They had matted hair and split jeans, filthy jumpers and pierced noses, Doc Martens and trainers: squatters. The duty solicitor was calling out to see if anyone wanted free advice, ushers were shouting names, tenants were explaining why they had not paid their rent, and a gang of local authority housing officers were sharing a joke.

Veronica turned out to be a tall and leggy and rather beautiful African woman. She stood in front of Lara and talked enthusiastically about Jamie's boss without pausing for breath until she saw the tenant, Mrs MacDonald, a small, tired-looking woman who was probably Lara's age. They went and sat down next to her and listened as she tried to explain in her lilting Barbadian accent why her rent arrears were so high. Before long, she was taking pieces of paper out of the dirty carrier bag which rested on her knees and handing them to Veronica who handed them to Lara. These were wage slips, letters from the Housing Benefit office and bank statements. Lara felt sorry for her: she had three children and her husband had left her two weeks before. But her record of payment was frankly terrible and St Patrick's, the small housing association which Lara was representing, had reluctantly decided that she should go.

When the usher called them in, Mrs MacDonald went and sat on one side of the court room and Lara and Veronicia sat on the other. The Deputy-District Judge, who was reading the court file, ignored them all. She was wearing glasses with large frames, a charcoal grey suit with a gold broach on the lapel, and a white silk blouse with a crease in the collar. Lara thought that she was in her late 50s. As she read, she played with the heavy ring on her finger.

She evidently favoured what Jamie called *the arresting start*. 'I've read your application,' she said, addressing Mrs MacDonald in a deep rumbling voice which put Lara in mind of a collapsing building. 'Perhaps you could tell me why on earth you think I should allow you to continue living at the property?' She had, Lara noticed, a faint Welsh accent.

After a moment's silence, Mrs MacDonald began to explain, with lots of *you knows* and *at the end of the days* and with her eyes fixed firmly on the District Judge, why her arrears were so high, how she thought that her husband had been paying the rent.

'Wait a moment,' interrupted the District Judge as she peered at the rent statement on the desk. 'He hasn't been paying, has he?'

'No, Madam, that's right,' said Mrs MacDonald. 'You see,

he drinks.'

The District Judge stared at her. 'You knew he wasn't paying.'

'No, Madam, no,' said Mrs MacDonald in a quivering voice.

'You must have seen the rent statements?'

'We've had problems with the letters. The man he don't deliver.'

'No housing benefit payments, I see.'

'They stopped, I went down the Housing, there was a queue that went through the building, I waited all morning, they said …'

'But earlier you told me …'

And so it went on. Lara saw that the judge had no intention of conducting the hearing in the usual way: this was her court and she would cross-examine the applicant, thank you very much. She did this with little skill but much vigour. At times, Lara felt less like a lawyer at a county court than a spectator at an act of ritualised humiliation. The judge took no heed of the most basic rules of court etiquette: as Mrs MacDonald explained that her hours as an office cleaner had been cut back, she murmured 'I see, I see,' in such a mocking tone that Lara and Veronica looked at each other in surprise. And after Mrs MacDonald pointed out that her MP was writing to the Housing Benefit Department on her behalf, the judge tried to catch Lara's eye.

'I'm sure that will make all the difference,' she wittily said.

But Mrs MacDonald stood her ground: she seemed to draw upon reserves of dignity in a way which Lara could only admire. When, however, Mrs Macdonald tried to summarise her present situation, the judge interrupted her. 'Why should I believe you?'

'Because these the facts, Madam.'

The judge leaned across the table towards her and said with a wintry smile, 'I don't think that you're telling me the truth.'

That struck Lara as unfair. Mrs MacDonald hadn't explained everything, but the judge had no evidence before her that she was telling lies.

'I see that this is your fourth stay application,' said the judge. 'You're wasting everyone's time, aren't you?'

'No,' said Mrs MacDonald, shrinking back in her chair.

The judge smiled at Lara, 'Miss Malkova, I needn't trouble you.' She turned back towards Mrs MacDonald, and as she stared at her in silence, the only sound Lara could hear was the scratching of Veronica's biro. 'Application dismissed. The eviction will proceed,' the judge barked, clenching the fingers of her left hand before stretching them again.

'What about my children, I mean, Christmas?' asked Mrs MacDonald, so quietly that Lara could only just make out what she was saying.

The judge took off her glasses to reveal pale patches around her eyes. 'Not sure if you've done right by your children,' she said as she typed out the order. Mrs MacDonald flinched as if she had been hit, and for a moment Lara thought the woman was going to cry. Lara was used to seeing tears in court but this felt different. She'd never heard a judge speak to a party like that before. She'd seen judges shout at counsel, she'd seen them snap at witnesses, she'd seen stupid judges and sleepy judges, pompous judges and lazy judges, and an awful lot of judges who didn't really care what happened one way or the other. But she hadn't seen a judge raise her sensible shoe and take a swing at someone on the floor like that. *Don't say anything,* she told herself. *Mrs MacDonald is about to lose her home so the comment of a judge is the last thing she'll worry about. Keep quiet, Lara, or you'll only make it worse.* On the other hand … how could it be worse? The poor woman had lost her husband, her home, and now this authority-figure was telling her that she was a bad mother.

'Madam,' said Lara, 'you should not have said that.'

The judge looked at Lara in amazement and Lara was herself amazed at what she had said. 'I beg your pardon?' said the judge, in a voice which had suddenly become higher, almost squeaky.

'I'm sorry, Madam,' said Lara, acutely conscious that everyone in the room was staring at her, 'but this hearing is about Mrs MacDonald's rent arrears and not about her qualities as a mother.'

'How dare you tell me what I can and cannot say?'

'I think it's important,' said Lara lamely.

'I'm surprised that someone of your call should talk to me like that. You may not have noticed but you're meant to be representing the Claimant.'

'That is not the point, Madam. With respect, Madam, none of us is in a position to judge … to judge …'

Veronica was writing furiously and out of the corner of her eye, Lara saw that the usher was nervously touching his earring.

'Don't raise your voice at me, Miss Malkova.'

'She didn't raise her voice,' said Mrs MacDonald, half-rising from her seat.

Veronica stopped writing and looked up. 'She didn't raise her voice.'

'Miss Malkova,' said the judge, looking Lara up and down, 'I will not tolerate rudeness from counsel. I will report you to the Ministry of Justice and to your, ah, regulatory body …'

'The Bar Standards Board,' said Lara.

'The Bar Standards Board. In the meantime,' she said, glaring at Lara, 'it would be best if you did not appear before me. Now will everyone please leave the court.'

'Court rise,' said the usher sounding relieved that it was over.

Outside the courtroom, Lara watched Mrs MacDonald walk slowly down the stairs with her head bowed, clutching her carrier bag in one hand and holding the banister with the other.

'I'm sorry, Veronica,' she said, 'I had to say something as that's exactly the sort of comment which can push people over the edge.'

'The judge won't forget it,' replied Veronica, wanting Lara to know that she was unhappy with what had happened but unwilling to say so directly.

Lara stepped back to let people pass on their way into the courtroom. 'The woman's a raving lunatic.'

'But to be perfectly honest, Lara, I'm slightly worried now. I've a load of these applications coming up. She'll take it out on us.'

'If she behaves unreasonably, then you appeal,' said Lara. 'You can talk to Jamie about that.'

'No, not Jamie, it's Andrew who I usually deal with. Jamie was just helping out, instructing you. I'd better go and call Andrew now. He won't be very happy with what's happened. But what are you going to do about her reporting you?'

'I'll speak to my Head of Chambers and see what he says,' said Lara. She had a good idea he would call her into his room and drone on as he wiped his glasses on his handkerchief. He would talk at her about the importance of courtesy at the bar. About respect for the Judiciary. About how she might want to be a judge herself one day – though she was probably too young to even think about that. About how she should write a letter of apology.

As Lara turned to go, she almost bumped into Mrs MacDonald, who had come back and seemed to be waiting for her with a friend. The friend had a small child hanging off each arm.

'This is Lisa,' she said, 'she looks after the kids when I'm at work. She came to help me today. I'm going to the Housing now. Thank you – it wasn't your fault, you know that. We get things wrong, don't we?' She walked away quickly before Lara could think of anything to say.

In the robing room, Lara thought of calling Georgie and asking her advice. So she quickly stuffed her brief into her bag, took out her iPhone and scrolled down her contacts until she found Georgie's name. But then she stopped as she knew who she wanted to speak to and it wasn't Georgie.

When she told him what had happened, he said that he would write to the Ministry of Justice to complain about the Judge and that Lara should do the same.

'So you don't think I should retire?' she asked.

'Not just yet.'

'Or become a solicitor?'

'Definitely not. You should have a word with your head of chambers.'

'Jamie,' she interrupted. 'Wasn't it awful?'

'Yes, and you should make a careful note of exactly what was said. There's obviously no need to contact your insurers.'

'Jamie,' she said, 'I don't want your advice. I want you to say "Poor old you."'

'Poor old you.'

'No, Jamie, for God's sake, not just repeat it.'

'Poor old you. But Lara, I really do mean it.'

Before she left the robing room, she looked in the mirror.

She hadn't cried and she was proud of that, at least, but my God she seemed old. The lines under her eyes were more distinct than she remembered them to be and her skin looked dry. She'd never seen the likeness before but now she couldn't deny it. She looked like her mother in the photo which she kept in her jewellery box, the one taken a few days before she died.

20th December

LARA HAD BEEN SITTING at the kitchen table making lists for an hour and not getting very far. But she was pleased that she had something to distract her. Christmas Lists and other Lists: Poppy's Christmas present: dog, jeans, camera. She crossed out jeans and camera and, using a squiggly arrow, inserted dog-lead and dog-basket. Adding an asterisk, she wrote: 'Check with Jamie about Dog!!! Christmas Day go to church.' She put a line through 'go to church.' She was conscious of a sense of satisfaction which even these inadequate lists gave her. These lists, she knew, had an eerie resemblance to the first lists, the lists which kicked-started her list-habit: the lists she put together as she prepared for her Bar Finals. Then she would create lists of cases, lists of topics, lists of principles, lists of rules, and once, day of days, a List of Lists, all of which she would stick over her bedroom walls. These lists had the same wonky double underlinings, the same use of roman numerals and the same somewhat prissy use of commas.

Now the kitchen was becoming so dark that she was finding it difficult to read her spidery handwriting. She crossed through all the lists and dropped the Bic on the table and watched it bounce. This time last year she could never have predicted that they would end up like this. She would give up making lists. She would give up trying to plan everything. She had spent most of her working life pretending that there is one answer, and now she knew that was not true. She could not decide what her clients should be doing, and she could not decide what *she* should be doing.

All she knew was that she wanted to see Jamie. If she was not going to be serious then she wanted not to be serious with him. How many people were there whom she could talk nonsense with as she could with Jamie? As much as she loved Amanda and Georgie and her other friends, there really was no competition. She remembered the years before Poppy was born, how they would talk nonsense for hours and hours, only stopping for sex and sometimes not even then. Really, she missed the nonsense, that daily holiday from logic, more than anything else. At work, she had to make sense, she understood that, it was what she was paid for. Being with Jamie was when she could forget the need to be reasonable and the need to justify every statement she made. She couldn't live without that, she just couldn't.

She heard a car pull up outside, walked towards the window and watched Georgie slam the car door shut. *Damn. Damn. Damn.* She'd forgotten that they had arranged this meeting.

Five minutes later, Georgie, immaculate in her navy-blue Nicole Farhi suit, was doodling on the back of Lara's Lists whilst Lara put coffee into the Italian coffee pot she and Jamie had bought in Florence. After she had lit the gas, she turned round to see that Georgie was looking at her disapprovingly.

'Come on sweetheart,' said Georgie, 'we've got to nail this.' On the table lay a photocopy of an article from the *Family Law Journal*.

'This is a bad idea, Georgie.'

'Lara,' said Georgie, standing up, 'he won't have a prayer.' She began to walk around the kitchen and as she walked she suggested arguments which Jamie would come up with and explained how Lara could shoot them down.

It was quite a performance, but when Lara told Georgie that she was being grotesquely unfair to Jamie, Georgie raised her eyes to the ceiling. 'Please don't worry, Lara, it won't be that bad. There's a lot of rubbish spoken about how stressful litigation is but I reckon people usually enjoy themselves. It releases their aggression,' said Georgie whose Christmas present from Giles last year had been a place on an anger-management course. 'The hearing won't take long,' she added. 'Half a day at First Avenue House and after that we can celebrate.'

Lara found herself wondering how someone of Georgie's phenomenal intelligence – she had a double first and all that – could fail to understand that this could not be one more piece of litigation to talk about in Daly's over a bottle of champagne.

'Celebrate? You think that this could be a matter for celebration?'

'Of course. You used to say that he would always put work before you and Poppy. Nothing's changed. Come on, Lara, you know the law here better than I do …'

'Sod the effing law,' said Lara, quite loudly. 'This family should be able to agree without going to bloody court, and if that means that Poppy lives with Jamie for half the week then so be it.'

Georgie shook her head sadly. 'Is that it?'

'Yes, yes it is,' she said, trying really hard not to cry.

'Where does that leave you?'

'It doesn't matter where it leaves me.'

'No, Lara, no. If you want to be a good mother, you'll fight him.'

'Georgie, you don't understand.'

Georgie stood up and folded her arms. 'Lara, he's a

numero-uno bastard, he's a pisshead, he's lazy – you said he used to spend half the weekend on the sofa listening to opera – he's not interested in Poppy, this is one more bloke who wants to get his own way.' She waited a moment and then said, 'And, by the way, all those words are your words, Lara.'

It was then that Poppy appeared. She must have been listening at the door. 'Don't you talk about my dad like that, you horrible woman,' she screamed in a voice which Lara had never heard before. 'He *is* interested in me and he's *not* lazy. He gets tired, he works far too hard and *you're* the one who drinks too much. You were drunk at the book club, I could hear you from upstairs.'

When Georgie laughed in Poppy's face, Lara pushed her towards the door. 'Just get out will you, just go.'

Georgie's freckly face reddened. 'Don't you dare touch me. Who the hell do you think you are? What are you going to do? Set your borzoi hounds on me?'

'Just go!' shouted Poppy. 'Go!'

Georgie stood still for a moment as if making a point. 'I will see myself out,' she said calmly.

Lara and Poppy stared at each other as they listened to Georgie's steps in the hall and the sound of the door being slammed.

'I'm sorry, Mum,' Poppy whispered, as if Georgie was still listening, 'I'm really sorry.'

'Darling,' said Lara, putting her hands on Poppy's shoulders, 'you're the only one who doesn't have to apologise. You know, I've never said that I'm sorry about what's been happening over the last year. I don't know why it happened, I just don't know. But I can't imagine that Dad has apologised either. The thing is, when you get older …'

'He has, actually,' said Poppy softly. 'It was rather sweet.'

21st December

LARA USED TO VISIT her mother every Christmas but when she saw how overgrown the graveyard had become she remembered that she hadn't been there for the last two years. Some of the gravestones were covered with long grass, and there were brambles around the Victorian angel at the far end. It was as if the present was making every effort to cover up the past. There was ivy on the yew tree. Weeds grew on the gravel path which wound its way around the thirteenth-century Sussex flint church with whitewashed walls where her mother had occasionally sung in the choir as a girl. 'Small and lonely in a field beneath the Downs' was how Betjeman had described the church. The families of sheep on the other side of the fence seemed to be watching her as she pushed open the door. There was no one inside. The silence, she remembered, seemed to have its own particular sound. She took off her scarf and sat down on the same pew on which she always sat and made the same prayer for the same two persons as she always made to the God in whom she did not believe.

From the porch outside she could see over the sheep the Sussex village where her mother had lived. The only sound was the distant hum of traffic on the A272. It was that time of the day in winter, half an hour or so before sunset, when everything seems to slow down. Beside her mother's grave was a vase of rotting stalks, and for a moment Lara wondered if someone else had been visiting. But her mother had no family other than herself and Lara's father, and he never came. They were, she realised, the remains of the flowers she had brought when she was last here. She emptied the vase and filled it with fresh water from the tap at the back of the church. She pushed in the roses she'd bought at the supermarket, put the vase back by the grave and stood there for a few minutes.

She remembered how as a teenager she would stand in the same place and cry. At the time she didn't really know why she cried. When she saw her friends with their mothers, she missed having a mother, and when she argued with her father, and she spent quite a lot of time arguing with her father, she missed her mother even more. In her early 20s, confident and harsh in her condemnations, Lara would think of her teenage self as self-pitying and confused. For how could she mourn someone she could hardly remember? Her mother had died shortly before Lara's third birthday. All she could remember of her was a feeling of warmth. But now, as she stood in silence and felt the coldness of December on her face, those feelings seemed perfectly understandable. What could be more natural than a child wanting a parent?

On the way home, Lara thought that she would try and avoid Guildford and she programmed her satnav accordingly. As she drove, she found herself thinking about what Jamie had said in La Stella: that she was 'possessive' and that this had something to do with her mother dying; and that, during their time together, he had felt excluded, and that this made life impossible or something like that. He was a bit vague on the details, a bit vague as to what caused what. But what seemed to be happening here was that he had found himself a Why It Went Wrong Theory or at least One Reason Why It Went Wrong. Every ex needs one, of course: a theory as to why he or she is an ex. Nowadays, it is never enough to say that the other person was cold/violent/unfaithful/always drunk. In Lara's circle at least, the theory would usually contain one or more quasi-technical term: in the last couple of years, Lara had heard one ex described as 'narcissistic,' another as a 'sociopath,' and two as 'on the spectrum.' However, all that was by the by. She didn't need a fancy theory to know that at times she had failed Jamie and that at times Jamie had failed her. As to why what happened happened, she really didn't know and it no longer seemed important that she should know.

Lara was so busy thinking about Jamie that she missed the prompt of her satnav and went straight on instead of turning left. In her headlights she thought she saw seagulls on a village green. Where was she? Oh, God … But Sean, the Irish voice on her satnav, didn't shout, he didn't complain, he didn't get cross. He didn't say, 'Well, that's it! We might as well give up!' Instead, he waited a moment, perhaps so he could get his bearings, perhaps so she could calm down, and then gave new directions, or as she liked to think of it, new suggestions, to take them to where they were going.

22nd December

ARCHIE WAS IN BED reading for the tenth time Benedict's practical if somewhat charmless two-line resignation email when he heard the doorbell ring. Paulo, he thought, it had to be Paulo. Whenever the doorbell rang it had to be Paulo. Whenever Meg received a text, it had to be Paulo. She had been looking so distracted over the last few days. She was probably dressed and waiting for him. His Meg was leaving home again.

The doorbell rang twice as he went down the stairs, muttering, 'Alright, alright.' When he undid the chain and opened the door he found himself smiling. He'd never met Paulo but he was pretty sure that he wouldn't be in his 20s and wearing a cycling helmet.

'Are you Archie Winterbourne?'

'Yes,' Archie mumbled. 'It's a bit early for Christmas carols.'

The man ignored that and handed Archie a large white envelope marked with his name in capital letters. 'This is an Order from the court,' he said with an air of weariness. 'If you do not understand it, then you should take legal advice.' He turned on his heel and walked away in long lolloping strides.

'Who's that?' called out Meg from the top of the stairs.

'Just a delivery, Meg. You go back to bed. Would you like me to bring you a cup of tea?'

'No, I'll come down. I'd rather have it with you, I'll be one minute.'

Tea with him? He was surprised. Over the last few days Meg had spent so long in her room that at times he almost forgot that she was still in the house. He hurried into the kitchen and tore open the envelope with a sense of shame that made him want to hide in a corner. He knew damn well what the Order was about and he was right. The Order required him not to harass or intimidate Ms Saint Ledger or he could be fined or imprisoned. There would be another hearing in three weeks. This was so unfair. Where could he find legal advice over Christmas? In any case, he had done nothing wrong, nothing at all. He'd tried hard to make sure that Benedict behaved properly. Thank you so very much Benedict.

Meg was at the door wearing her pink linen dressing gown and her silk slippers. 'Can I come in? Should I shut my eyes?'

Archie stuffed the Order back in the envelope and put it in the table drawer. 'No, there's no need for that. You know me,' he said with a transparently fraudulent laugh, 'I've nothing to hide.'

She grinned. 'I'll make the tea, Archie, you've been working so hard. Oh yes, I bought some croissants yesterday.'

He watched her as she filled the kettle, take the croissants out of the cupboard and put them in the microwave. He'd never seen her so happy. She was actually humming a tune, something he'd never heard before. When was he going to tell her about the flat? Before lunch? During lunch? After lunch? Now. He took a deep breath. 'Meg, Benedict's resigned. He been acting like a complete madman.'

She turned round to look at him. 'I know,' she said calmly as she put the croissants on a plate.

Archie couldn't believe it. 'You know? How do you know?'

She put two tea bags in the pot which, having long since mastered the dramatic pause, she filled before she spoke. 'He called me yesterday and told me what he's been doing. Stupid little idiot. He's been phoning her and sending her postcards, telling her to get out. He actually thought it funny. That poor woman. I said if he didn't resign, he'd be sacked. I think that he did it on purpose. He wanted to be sacked. He once told me that he thought he shouldn't have to work, that his parents should look after him. Taking him on was a big mistake, Archie. I blame myself. I thought he was just what you needed.'

'It wasn't your fault, Meg. I think it's impossible to tell what people are really like.' He hoped she didn't think he was referring to Paulo. 'I should have managed him more carefully. I just let him get on with things. I'll go and see her, the tenant, I mean, to apologise. Yes?'

Meg didn't answer immediately. She was making him wait again. She took two plates out of the cupboard and put them on the table. To these she added knives, two mugs and the teapot. 'A really good letter would be better,' was what she finally said. 'I'll draft something. We'll explain that the business has not been properly managed, and that we're going to offer her compensation and of course payment of her costs.'

'Costs? Are you sure?'

'Absolutely sure,' she said, nodding her head. 'The Law Centre is unlikely to settle otherwise.'

'Ok.'

'And as for Benedict leaving – that might suit us,' she said in a businesslike way.

'Us?'

'You and me, Archie,' she said so quietly that he found himself tilting his head towards her. 'You wouldn't mind,' she asked, 'if I had my old job back, would you?'

'That might make sense,' he said in a serious professional

tone as his heart sang for joy at the prospect of seeing Meg, his Meg, regularly. 'To be honest, it's all been a bit of a mess since you left.'

'I think that's an understatement, Archie. Benedict has done virtually nothing. He's been taking you for a ride.'

'That bad?'

'That bad.'

'Sorry. I think I lost interest,' he said. Without you, he thought, nothing really mattered.

'Don't worry, Archie,' she said, reassuringly. 'We'll have everything back on track in no time.'

He had to say it. 'But the flat in Wimbledon, I won't be able to pay you – you'll lose it. You'll need to let Toby know.'

'That's ok,' she said. 'We can stay here, can't we?'

'Of course you can, Meg, but I wasn't thinking of going anywhere.'

'We, Archie, we,' she said, smiling again in a way which he'd never seen her smile, she was almost a different person.

'Yes,' he said, not sure what she was actually saying and even wondering for a truly horrible moment if she meant that Paulo would turn up with a suitcase having lost all his money. 'Of course we can stay here. I know that people say Clapham is a bit rough, there's a lot of social housing but people have to live somewhere. I think that there's nowhere quite like it. I suppose that the Common is part of the answer and of course the architecture, and its history. Lots of writers have lived here – *The End of the Affair* was set here …'

'We, Archie,' she said with an air of infinite patience as she walked round to his side of the table and picked up his hand and placed it on her tummy.

'We?'

'Yes.'

'What?'

'This,' she said pressing her hand over his hand.

'Your dressing gown? It's nice. I've always liked linen.'

'For God's sake, Archie.'

'Your stomach … you're not ill, are you?'

'No, I'm not ill. I'm pregnant.'

'You're pregnant?'

'Yes, I'm pregnant.'

'With a baby? You mean you're pregnant?'

'Yes.'

'I think I'd better sit down.'

'You are sitting down.'

'Yes, I am. When?'

'July, early I think.'

'You can't remember?'

'July next year. Are you ok?'

'No, I mean, when did you, er, how long have you been like this?'

'November. Please don't say "like this."'

'Sorry, I'm in a state of shock. But Paulo …'

'He doesn't know. I can guess what he'd want me to do.'

'No, you can't do that Megan, you can't do that. Promise me.'

She sat down on the chair next to him so that their knees were touching. She was making him wait for his answer again, as if everything this morning had to be thought out carefully.

'That's why I asked you for the money. It wasn't for the solicitor.'

'I know that, I called him. I thought it was for an airline ticket.'

'No, Archie,' she said, lowering her voice again, making

him wonder if he was going deaf.

'I don't want to see Paulo,' she said. 'I hope I never see him again.'

'Are you going to tell him?'

'It might be a girl.'

'I mean tell Paulo, Meg. Doesn't he have a right to know?'

'Not after the way he treated me. He can go to hell.'

'You want to stay here?'

She leaned forward and gently kissed a dumbfounded Archie on his dumbfounded lips.

'Of course I want to stay here. It's my home.'

Home. 'But you went away. You never contacted me. You didn't even send me a Christmas card.'

'People don't send Christmas cards nowadays, Archie.'

'No, I suppose they don't.'

For a moment there was silence and then she said, 'I made a mistake.'

'Not contacting me?'

'No, you dope, leaving here.'

'You mean leaving me.'

'I mean you, yes.'

'How do I know you won't make another mistake?'

'That's a fair question, Archie.'

'Then it deserves a fair answer.'

'I missed you. I didn't know how much I would miss you.'

'That's not terribly reassuring, Meg.'

'I belong here.'

'You mean with me.'

An infinitesimal pause is still a pause. 'With you, yes,' she said, 'with you.'

'What are you going to tell her or him?'

'I don't know. That's a long way away. We can discuss it

nearer the time.'

'I think I need to know. I need to understand how I'll fit in.'

'Fit in, Archie? He or she will love you, Archie, that's how you'll fit in.'

He had to say it. 'You never wanted a baby when you were with me.'

'It didn't feel right. I was very young. How old was I when we met – 25? I was just a girl.'

'But you feel different now?'

'Totally. Perhaps one day, we can have another.'

'Steady on, you haven't had this one yet.'

'*We* haven't had this one yet,' she said with a little frown before standing up and starting to put the breakfast things away, that very ordinary thing you do at home.

She had, he remembered, made excuse after excuse. It had never been the right time. But what mattered was now, not how things were. The child would be their child, that is what mattered, that is all that mattered. Other things – what happened, when, where, with whom –were mere facts, and they were facts which didn't matter.

23rd December

LARA SLIPPED HER NEW recording of *Eugene Onegin* into the CD player and flopped down on the sofa. Jamie was coming over. He had, he said, some news, and so she had spent the last hour cleaning the kitchen and choosing what to wear. She knew that in the circumstances both activities were absurd but absurdity had been the theme of the year and she no longer cared. The kitchen was clean enough and the stripey grey and blue jumper and black jeans she was wearing would be perfectly alright.

Poppy, her usual source of advice with regard to clothes, was out shopping with Jess. That was a shame as she would have liked to see Jamie and Jamie would have liked to see her. But they would see each other at Amanda's Christmas Party tomorrow. After that, Poppy would spend the evening and Christmas morning with her and the rest of Christmas Day and Boxing Day with Jamie. Such were this year's arrangements. *The St Lucie's Day Agreement*, Jamie called it. Not once during her discussions with Poppy about Christmas had Poppy been anything other than cheerful and sensible. Truly, thought Lara, as the overture came to its surprising end, they did not deserve her.

When she opened the door, she thought for a moment that Jamie's hair had turned white, as if he was returning to the house not after a year but after a lifetime.

In the kitchen, he went over to look at the photos on the fridge door. 'These are new,' he said. There was one of her looking a fright at Amanda's, and one of Poppy in the garden, and one of her and Poppy eating ice cream on the beach at West Wittering. 'Where was this taken?' he asked.

She told him. 'Don't you recognise it?'

'When did you go?' he asked, somewhat abruptly, as if he should have been invited too.

The year had been so long and so strange that she had to think hard. 'July, I think. Possibly August.'

'Ok.'

'Would you like a cup of coffee?' she asked, thinking how strange that conventional question sounded in their kitchen.

'Please,' he said, glancing out of the window before looking at the floor. He was, she thought, doing everything he could not to look at her.

When she had made them coffee, she leaned back against the stove and looked at him. He was wearing a green check shirt which she hadn't seen before and his old pale blue Levis.

'I can't stay long,' he said. He had just arrived but he was already talking about leaving, as if leaving had become his natural mode.

She kept her expression blank. 'I thought you had the day off?'

'I'm meeting Anaïs.'

Anaïs. Yes of course. Perhaps they would do their Christmas shopping in the King's Road, starting with coffee and croissants in Sloane Square. Lunch at Colbert? What could be more romantic? She knew that it was romantic because that was what she and Jamie and Poppy used to do.

'Shopping?' she asked.

He seemed to find that amusing. 'No,' he said before explaining that the Law Centre had obtained an injunction to stop Anaïs's downstairs neighbours harassing her. It was, he said, a pretty obvious case of racism. Anaïs was from West Africa and the neighbours weren't. Some of their language was horrible. The middle classes think that everyone has moved on but that is not the case at all. Her large housing association was as useless as large housing associations invariably are, and the same could be said about the police. As he told her about the latest outrage, she remembered how he had sat in that chair and spoken about other cases and other injunctions. When he felt strongly about a case, when he felt strongly about anything, he always gave his everything, and that was one of the things she loved about him. Most of the solicitors who instructed her were interested in little else but money. She sometimes thought that a visitor from outer space might report back that as well as human beings planet earth was inhabited by creatures called 'solicitors' who for the most part looked liked human beings but who could not open their mouths without using the word 'costs'.

'You like her, don't you?' she teased.

'Not in that way,' he said unconvincingly. 'I feel a bit sorry for her, that's all.'

'Mmmm.'

'What does that mean?'

'It just means mmmm.'

But that wasn't quite true. Mmmm meant that when Poppy had come home on Sunday she had mentioned that Jamie had spent a lot of time texting someone and mmmm also meant that Jamie himself had told her stories of how at times he had been given to confusing feeling sorry for a person with loving them.

'How was the opera?' he asked abruptly, as if he needed to change the subject before saying too much.

'Wonderful. I think I'm a convert.' She found herself telling him how she met Michael, who knew even less about opera than she did. Jamie showed no reaction to that. But when she told him how she had remembered an aria which he used to play when they were decorating their flat in Hackney, a remark which she had thought long and hard about making, his reaction surprised her.

'I can't listen to opera anymore,' he said with an air of quiet despair, reminding her for some reason of a Graham Greene character admitting he could no longer pray. 'I spend most of my time listening to Shostakovich,' he added with a pretty good attempt at a Russian pronunciation of the name, not something she'd ever heard him try before.

'Really?' she gulped.

He nodded his head slowly. 'The other week I heard Building a Library compare different recordings of *Figaro*. I listened to it three times and after that, I played my Jacobs recording all weekend. Enough,' he said, raising his hands in a somewhat operatic gesture. 'Enough for a lifetime.'

Finishing his coffee, he stood up.

'Jamie, I think that you're exaggerating. Don't go.'

'There's something else,' he said, obediently sitting down again. 'I think I've been using opera to block out life or as a substitute for life, I'm not sure which. You know I never really told you how unhappy I was at work, I felt too embarrassed. I couldn't talk to anyone about it, so part of the time I just lived this unreal life through opera. That's not how to live and it's not how to enjoy opera either. The obvious comparison is with being boozed or drugged out. It wasn't fair on you, I'm really sorry, Lara. Anyway,' he said, looking away, 'now's not the time.'

Now seemed a good time to her. 'Would you like a drink?'

'Thanks but no.'

'But you're happy now?'

'I'm happy,' he said with a radiant smile. 'I'm happy because 'I've handed in my notice.'

'What? Was that because of the St Patrick's hearing?'

'No, of course not. Andrew was not a happy bunny but I'd made up my mind by then. I should have done it years ago.'

'Where do you think you'll go?'

He smiled. 'Where do you think?'

She named a firm, well known for its human rights work, which he had mentioned in the past.

'Definitely not.'

She named another which she knew instructed her chambers and had swanky offices in Clerkenwell.

'No way,' he said.

'You are kidding,' was his response to her third suggestion and, 'I'd rather be dead in a field' to her fourth. She liked his responses and wondered if he was beginning, perhaps, to talk to her with the same lack of formality which they had had when they were together, as if he was beginning to feel at home.

'So where then?

'Nowhere. I wasn't meant to be a solicitor, Lara. I've applied for a place on a PGCE course.'

'Seriously?' she asked, thinking at once that she'd said the wrong thing.

'Yes,' he said, not taking any offence and in fact looking happier than she'd seen him look in years. 'At Strawberry Hill, you know, next to Horace Walpole's house. I have my Eng. Lit. degree already – I'm going to teach English, Lara. I'll be older than most of my fellow students but not all of them.'

'Have you told Poppy?

'Yes.'

'You told Poppy and not me?'

'You've been busy,' he said pointedly, 'and she's been

putting up with me wittering on about books for years. Look,' he said, glancing up at their kitchen clock, 'I really do have to go now. Thanks for the coffee.'

She was about to tell him that he couldn't just go off after such an announcement, that her practice was hardly blooming, that without his salary they would not be able to pay the mortgage, let alone his rent as well. But she stopped herself, knowing that this was not the time for that. He had arrived in a state of gloom and now he was smiling and that was good.

She followed him to the front door and felt the rush of cold air. It had been snowing hard again, his footprints on the path had vanished. She had that giddy sensation she often had when it snowed: that the world was burying her mistakes and allowing her to make a fresh start. The roofs on the houses opposite looked like blank pieces of paper. This is where we are, the world seemed to be saying, try again. For what seemed like ages the two of them stood together sharing the sight of this ordinary suburban street now glowing in whiteness. 'It's so beautiful,' he said, turning to look at her with glistening eyes.

Without saying more, he walked down the path towards his car and as she watched him, she found herself noticing of all things how much weight he had lost. When she had first met him, he had a kind of animal sleekness which she thought had gone for ever. But it had returned. He stopped at the gate and looked at her as though he was going to say something. But he closed the gate, got into the car and fastened the seatbelt with that gauche way of moving which he had. He was so awkward, but she had seen so little of him recently that she had almost forgotten that basic fact about him. She waited for him to lower the window as he always used to when she stood there watching, so that they could have one last exchange before he went wherever he was going. But the window stayed closed, and the car began to move slowly over the snow-covered road. She wanted it to stop, she wanted to say more, though she wasn't sure what. Why didn't it stop? Wouldn't the snow stop it? He often forgot something and came back. But after a few seconds, the car disappeared from sight.

24th December

LARA HAD SPOTTED HIM in the kitchen soon after she'd arrived. He was tall, almost perfectly bald, and very good-looking. When he saw that she was alone, he came over and introduced himself. He was either from Australia or New Zealand, she wasn't sure which. She felt a sense of relief that she wasn't the only guest who wasn't part of a couple. From where she was standing she could see an Asian couple and an African couple, a tall couple and a short couple, a thin couple who sounded as if they were American, and standing by the door, Amanda's parents – who seemed oppressively coupley, even to the extent of periodically touching each other's arms.

He was now leaning towards Lara and smiling. 'I think that relationships are a bit like cricket matches.'

'You mean dangerous?'

'No,' he said, as he raised his sparse eyebrows to indicate that he was pleased with his answer, 'they are often at their most interesting when nothing obvious is happening.'

'Not sure if I want to be in an interesting relationship,' she said, thinking as she spoke how boring she must sound and wondering when she had become boring or whether she had always been boring.

He stared at her empty glass as if he was thinking along the same lines. 'Can I get you some more champagne?' He was drinking orange juice, which could mean that he was an alcoholic; it could mean many things, not that she was interested in him. She couldn't imagine being interested in anyone again, but she always worked on the principle that you really can't have too much attention.

'Please,' she said.

Amanda crept towards her. 'So you've met Alan?' she whispered.

'Yes,' she said, giving a little excited and dishonest smile.

'Isn't he nice?'

Lara nodded. 'Your kitchen,' she said, looking around the room. 'It's changed.' There was now only one photo of Rob and gone too were the photos of Rob's sculpture.

'I thought it time,' said Amanda as the doorbell rang. 'I went to Georgie's last night and we talked about Rob and I didn't cry. I didn't even feel like crying. So when I came home, I put the kitchen back to how it used to be without really thinking about it. Rob will always be with me,' she said, putting her glass on the mantelpiece. 'I don't need to make the kitchen look weird to know that.'

'Fab,' said Lara, not wanting to let on how amazed she was. She'd sometime thought that Amanda would never get over Rob.

'Progress, yes. By the way,' said Amanda as Alan trotted back with a glass of champagne, 'Jamie called to say that he'll be late.'

'That's a shame,' said Lara as casually as she could. Why hadn't he told her? But then, why should he?

'This one's an example to us all, Alan,' said Amanda. 'She and Jamie were at each other's throats and now they're getting on really well.'

'That's an exaggeration,' said Lara.

Alan leaned towards Lara again. 'Is Jamie the bloke who's been advising Anaïs?'

'That's right,' said Lara. 'He does voluntary work at Brixton Advice Centre. How do you know Anaïs?'

'She's my fiancée. I've been stuck in Melbourne for a month with Covid. That Jamie, he's a real miracle worker, you should be proud of him. I hope you'll both come to our wedding?'

***

'Lovely to see you,' said Amanda, as she kissed Meg at the door. 'Happy Christmas, Archie.'

'Happy Christmas to you,' said Archie, letting go of Meg's hand. 'Do you still need me, Amanda?'

'Need you for what?' asked Meg.

'I'm short of a Father Christmas,' said Amanda as they watched two small children chasing a third into the kitchen. 'Rob was our Father Christmas.'

Archie glanced at Meg. 'I don't have much experience of children, Amanda. Wouldn't you be better off with someone else?'

'Oh come on, Archie,' said Meg. 'I know you'll be amazing. Where's his outfit?'

'I left it on my bed, but have a drink first,' said Amanda, leading them into a room so noisy that Archie could hardly hear himself think. The kilims were stacked at one end of the room. At the other end was a table with a white cloth on which stood a line of champagne bottles set behind a row of glasses and a large jug filled with orange juice.

'So what did Meg give you for Christmas, Archie?' asked Amanda.

Archie looked at Meg and Meg looked at Archie. 'A secret present,' he said, smiling as he'd never smiled before.

Amanda was intrigued. 'What was it?'

Archie and Meg both shook their heads. 'I can't tell you, Amanda,' he said, wanting to tell her and everyone.

'Was it drugs?' whispered Amanda.

***

When Lara came into the kitchen, she saw Archie dressed as Father Christmas sitting on Amanda's non-rocking rocking chair listening with an of fascination to a small boy talking nonsense.

On the other side of the room, Georgie and Giles were standing by the fridge. Giles was wearing blue corduroys and a different sports jacket with leather patches at the elbows. In a red skirt and jumper and black leggings, Georgie looked like a fabulous bird. 'Thanks for your text,' she said as Lara kissed her. 'I'm so sorry for everything.'

'That's ok. You were only trying to help. Poppy loved her present, by the way. That was very kind.'

'Lara, it was the least I could do.'

'I didn't get into the college I applied for,' said Giles as Lara kissed him.

'Sorry to hear that.'

'I told him that he was too old,' said Georgie.

'But there's still a chance, another one might want me,' he said. 'We have to believe in miracles, don't we, Lara?'

'Don't go there, Lara,' said Georgie. 'I find that nowadays with Giles it's best to stick to facts and numbers. Anything else is just asking for trouble. He used to be good with numbers, especially zeros.'

'I don't want a miracle,' said Lara. 'I just want things to go a bit right. But you don't really believe in miracles, do you Giles?'

'We had an argument about miracles last week,' said Georgie.

'Another argument,' said Giles.

'It was bigger than usual.'

'No, it wasn't.'

'Of course it was.'

'Do you know what I did?' asked Georgie.

'Listen to what she did. She's shameless.'

'I'd been drinking.'

'She's always been drinking.'

'He had it coming.'

'Listen, Lara, listen to this.'

'I found one of his books.'

'One of my philosophy books, in the kitchen.'

'I tried to read it.'

'She could hardly stand.'

'The book contained no numbers and no facts, did it Giles?'

'This is what I have to put up with, Lara.'

'So I employed my new principle.'

'What's that?' asked Lara.

'If a book has no numbers and no facts then it must be nonsense,' said Georgie.

'She's causing havoc with my library. Do you know what she did?'

'Guess what I did.'

'What did you do?' asked Lara

'She put it in the log burner.'

'It burnt quite nicely.'

'What was it?' asked Lara.

'Can't remember,' said Georgie. 'But I'd stick to logs if I were you. Expensive way to heat the house.'

'Hello, Poppy, yes please,' said Georgie as she held her glass under the bottle of Lanson which Poppy was holding. 'Thank you, sweetheart.'

'Giles, you haven't told me if you believe in miracles,' said Lara.

'Lara,' groaned Georgie, 'he's been talking about effing miracles all morning.'

'I think,' said Giles, 'that there are miracles and there are miracles.'

'Here we go,' said Georgie.

'Please Georgie,' said Giles, as if he was speaking to a difficult child, which in a way he was.

'What do you mean, Giles?' asked Lara.

'The conventional idea of a miracle,' said Giles, 'is a breach in nature's laws, an event which can only be explained through reference to God.'

'Like the Star of Bethlehem,' said Lara.

'Yes,' he said. 'Or kneeling oxen, or the Virgin Birth, or talking angels.'

'What other kind of miracles are there?' asked Lara.

'Well,' began Giles as he reached into his jacket pocket and took out his pouch of tobacco. Georgie poked him with a long pale finger. 'Don't you dare light that pipe, Giles.'

'We also use the term,' said Giles with an air of studied patience, 'to describe something utterly extraordinary which we cannot begin to explain.'

'You mean,' said Georgie, 'we haven't yet found the scientific answer. But that's not a miracle, that's called not knowing the answer. I'm sure that a few hundred years ago, there would have been lots of things that we now take for granted which no one could have explained.'

Lara was surprised to see that Poppy was listening to this conversation and even more surprised to see Giles take hold of Poppy's shoulders. 'Do you mind if I use you?' he whispered in her ear. Poppy shook her head and Giles gently turned Poppy towards Lara. 'You remember when you first saw her?' Lara nodded. 'She would have looked partly like Jamie and partly like you. Correct?'

Georgie frowned. 'That's genes, Giles, that's not a miracle. Jesus.'

'That her nose was just as it was, that her eyes were just as they were. You would have known that there is, in theory, a complete genetic explanation of her appearance but I bet you still found it a miracle.'

'Don't you worry, Poppy,' said Georgie. 'He's reached middle age.'

'A complete explanation,' said Giles, 'would have to go back to the beginning of time. It would have to include all her ancestors, it would have to explain what came before them and why everything had to be as it had to be.'

'That makes me feel giddy,' said Lara.

'It would have to include an explanation of why there's anything at all. And we don't have that. Every theory starts with something.'

Poppy twisted round to look at him. 'Like the Big Bang theory?'

'That's it. It assumes matter.'

'That's not science,' said Lara.

'Exactly,' said Giles.

'So you do believe in miracles,' said Lara quietly.

'We all do,' said Giles, 'we just convince ourselves that we don't. Religion doesn't help – it tries to take over our sense of wonder for its own purposes. But we have to believe in miracles, it's a condition of our sanity.'

'Poppy,' said Georgie, 'I think you're supposed to be the Christmas miracle.'

'Yeah, right.'

'Shepherd's pie, anyone?' Amanda was calling.

On the other side of the kitchen, a boy with frizzy blond hair threw a plastic dragon at Archie's feet. 'I don't want my present,' he said.

'If you don't like it, chum, then go and find yourself another Father Christmas,' said Archie. 'There are plenty of them around at this time of the year.'

Lara took hold of Giles's jacket and pulled him to one side. 'But what if you know that what you want won't happen?'

'Lara, we know next to nothing,' said Giles, smiling kindly.

***

'I like your jacket,' said Lara as she gave Jamie a quick kiss on each cheek. It was a dark grey worsted jacket with a fake pocket, thin lapels and buttons in the shape of blackberries.

'I bought it last January. At the time I thought of it as an investment,' said Jamie.

'Has it paid off?' asked Lara, moving back to allow people to come into the kitchen.

'Too soon to tell,' he teased.

For a moment, neither of them spoke, and Lara wondered if their relationship had been reduced to desultory chats about jackets. Is that what she had to look forward to?

'By the way,' he said, 'I'm sorry for being upset yesterday.' He said it as if he'd been thinking about little else.

'When?'

'When I came round. Don't tell me you've forgotten,' he said, sounding now almost cross that she hadn't taken note of his emotional weather.

She took a mini-mince pie from the table and made him wait. 'There's nothing to apologise for.'

'Being in the house again made me go a little mad.'

'Really?' she said, wiping her mouth with a napkin.

'Yes. Let me get you some more champagne,' he said, taking her glass and wandering off, just when he'd arrived.

'Carmel,' said Georgie, going over to speak to her youngest, 'I think Father Christmas has been very patient.' She winked at Archie. 'But it's time to give someone else a chance to meet him. He'll have to leave soon. If he spends too much time in Clapham, someone will steal his reindeer.'

'So what did you get for Christmas, Giles?' asked Jamie.

That was enough. Giles only had to mention his subscription to the *Spectator* and Jamie launched into a one-sided discussion of how he missed the opera reviews of the of the late Michael Tanner, leading Lara to think that Jamie hadn't lost all his interest in opera.

But then Amanda dragged her off to meet her parents and that was difficult because they'd spotted Jamie, and Amanda hadn't told them about the separation. As soon as she could, she made her way back to the kitchen in time to see Jamie and Poppy open the back door and go outside with Giles and Carmel. They wanted, Poppy said, to see if all the snow had melted. When they came back, she knew that something was wrong. Jamie was as white as the melting snow.

'I don't feel too good,' he said, frowning and smiling by turns, and putting his hand on the back of a chair. He seemed unsteady.

'Sit down here,' said Poppy. 'Is it what you were talking about? Have you got that pain?'

'What pain?' asked Lara.

Jamie began to breath quickly whilst every now and then holding his breath as if he was trying to control his breathing.

'It's his angina,' said Poppy.

'He has angina?'

'Yes, it's a recent thing,' said Poppy. 'We didn't want to worry you.'

Lara couldn't believe what she was hearing. 'Shall I call an ambulance?'

Jamie spoke. 'I'll be fine. I just have to rest.'

'Is the pain still there?' asked Poppy, putting her hand on Jamie's shoulder.

He nodded. He was beginning to slump.

'I'm going to call an ambulance,' said Lara.

'No,' said Poppy, 'that would take ages. Ask Giles to drive him in his Range Rover. Dad can lie in the back.'

'Which hospital?' asked Lara.

'St George's,' whispered Jamie.

'That's where he's seen a consultant,' said Poppy.

'Only once,' said Jamie. 'There's nothing to worry about.'

'You go with him, Mum.'

'Yes, yes,' said Lara, thinking for a moment that Jamie was going to die in front of her, that she had to keep her cool, that she had to be like Poppy.

She went into the next room and pulled Giles away from Georgie who had her arm around him.

'You leave my man alone,' said Georgie, grabbing Giles's other arm. 'Find your own.'

'Giles, Jamie's ill. He may be having a heart attack, or he may be about to have one. We want you to take him to St George's. Now, now, now.'

'Jesus, Mary and Joseph,' said Georgie. 'Giles, do as the woman asks.'

In the kitchen, Jamie was sitting upright and breathing regularly.

'Giles,' said Poppy, 'go and get the car and pull up outside.

Put the back seat down, let him lie down if he wants. We'll help him outside. Can you stand, Dad?'

'Yes, yes,' he said, rising from the chair. 'I'll be fine.'

But he didn't look fine.

25th December

THE GIRLFRIEND CAME WITH him,' said the student nurse.

'Oh yes,' said Dr Hussain, trying to sound interested as he typed. He had been on duty since 6am and he was desperate to get away. His parents had arrived from Pakistan the day before and they were already bickering with his wife Joanne. He felt that the remark his mother had made about the kitchen being dirty was uncalled for. But did Joanne have to remind her of the rat she'd seen on their honeymoon in Karachi?

'The patient asked me to text her. He said that his vision was blurry and he didn't want to make a mistake. It's in the notes,' she added, leaning over his shoulder.

Dr Hussain swayed away from her. 'Will you give me some room?' he snapped.

She stepped back quickly. 'But that was alright, wasn't it? I mean, the texting.'

'Texting on a patient's phone?' he said, taking his hands off the keyboard and sitting back in the ridiculously uncomfortable chair. She had blonde hair and bright green eyes and could not be more than 20.

'He seemed upset.'

'They're all upset at this time of year. That's Christmas for you.'

'So what should I have done?'

'Look, I'm sure it's ok,' he said, turning his chair round and smiling at her. 'You were doing him a favour.'

'Of course I was.'

***

The café at the hospital was more crowded than Lara would have thought possible on Christmas morning. She guessed that most of the tables were occupied by those who had come to A&E or were waiting for people in A&E. No one, save a boy of around 8 who was playing with a toy dog, looked that happy, which was hardly surprising in the circumstances. The decorations and the sound of Christmas carols added to the air of gloom: Lara sensed the falseness of an institution's efforts. Against that background, private dramas were being played out. A couple at the next table were both looking at Kindles: she showed him something on hers and for what seemed like a fraction of a second he pretended to be interested. But then he raised his eyebrows to the ceiling and he began to look irritated.

Jamie had texted her this morning that he would be out soon, and so she had left Poppy with Amanda and jumped in the car. She now found herself looking round the café for the nurse she had spoken to yesterday, though of course there was no reason why she should be here. Lara had told her what had happened and helped her fill out the admission form: that was easy, she had known almost everything from his place of birth to his allergies. When the nurse had asked them for a person the hospital should contact in an emergency, she gave her own name. And what was the relationship? 'Friend or Partner?'

'Friend,' said Lara quickly. But the nurse had smiled. It wouldn't be long, the smile seemed to say.

And now, when she looked up, there was Jamie standing beside her table with a plaster above his eye and a piece of tinsel in his hair which made it appear as if he was wearing a crown.

'I thought you'd be longer,' she said, carefully pushing a chair towards him.

He caught hold of its back and sat down. 'The nurse turned a blind eye and I sneaked out.' He pointed at the tinsel. 'She did this. You like it?'

'Jamie, what did they say?'

He pointed to his heart. 'My arteries have narrowed. Stress and smoking.'

'But you don't smoke.'

'I used to.'

'That was years ago.'

'Then perhaps stress was more important. They don't really know, it's all more or less guesswork.'

'So what are they going to do?'

'They want to give me stents, I have to come back in the New Year, probably in February.'

'Thank God. You looked terrible.'

'But I was wearing my new jacket.'

'You're always wearing something new nowadays. I thought you were trying to impress Anaïs.'

'That's funny. She has a fiancé.'

'So I hear. Who was it, then?'

'I'll leave you to guess that.'

What did that mean? 'I suppose we should go,' she said, not wanting to take the conversation further. But he said that he really wanted a cup of coffee and so she went and bought him one and when she returned he was reading an old newspaper.

'How's Poppy?' he asked as he stirred his coffee and glanced at the paper and then at a nurse who had sat down at the next table.

'She's worried about you. She's always worried about you,' said Lara. 'But apart from that, she's ok.'

After she had spoken there was that silence again, the silence she'd heard when they'd met at court. She didn't know if it was there because they had nothing to say or because they had too much to say. But he gave her an encouraging smile. 'I'm still seeing her later?' he asked.

'Yes, of course.'

'What are you doing?'

'I'll just chill out,' she said. 'I'm seeing Dad tomorrow.'

'Chill out? You mean you'll watch television?'

'Er, yes. I suppose so. I'm also re-reading the last book we discussed at the book club. You came round, do you remember?'

When he nodded, the tinsel slipped in front of his face, and he pushed it aside. 'Re-reading's good but I'm not sure if you should be doing that on Christmas Day. Why don't you invite Poppy and me over?'

She hesitated, wondering if he was feeling sorry for her. 'But you've probably prepared something for Poppy.'

'I'm not the greatest cook in the world,' he said for the hundredth time since she'd met him.

'No?' she responded as she always responded.

'But I can bring over my offerings.'

'Do you have a tree?' she asked.

'Yes,' he said. 'Poppy and I bought one at the weekend. Do you want me to bring that as well?'

She laughed. 'No, we have a tree in the usual place. You saw that. I was just thinking about your poor lonely tree.'

'I'm sure it will be fine,' he said. 'It's amazing what you can get used to.'

'You won't want to watch television.'

'I'm not perfect, Lara.'

'I think I know that now. But nor am I.'

'No?' he asked, frowning and pretending to think hard. 'I suppose not. Did you once think me perfect?'

'No, not really. You, me?'

'No, not really. It sounded nice, though.'

'Yes.'

He leaned towards her and the tinsel flopped down again. 'I guess we're making progress,' he said, brushing it aside.

Progress towards what she thought. 'I think so,' she said, finding it impossible not to smile.

'Is this our round-table discussion?' he asked.

She looked down at the square plastic table. 'It's not very round.'

'It's not very clean either. Do you want me to get a cloth?'

'No, of course not. It will do.'

'I haven't been to many round-table discussions,' he said.

'I've been to one on Zoom. Hang on, why are we bringing in round-table discussions? I thought I was the one who was always a lawyer? That's what you said.'

'I've said lots of things, Lara. Anyway, I want to make an admission.'

'Ok, that's allowed. I suppose you'll be a lawyer for a few more months.'

'Until September, I hope,' he said.

'Then you'll be happy?'

'At least I won't be a lawyer.'

'Before you make your admission,' she said, 'I'd like to make an offer.'

'Go on, then.'

'Poppy agrees that I can say that she can stay with you for half the week.' There, she had said it. She had given him everything he had asked for. But he wasn't even smiling.

He was taking the tinsel from his head and running is fingers through his hair and staring at her for long enough to make her feel strange.

'Well, come on, then,' she said, gesturing towards the other tables with a wave, 'we're all waiting. Your admission.'

At that, he looked around the café. The pair opposite had been joined by a woman with her baby.

'It doesn't make sense, it's not making either of us happy.'

'Is that your admission?'

'No.'

'What are you saying?'

'You know what I'm saying.'

'Are you talking about Poppy?'

'No, yes, I'm talking about us.'

'Us?'

'Us. You know, the pronoun. It refers to two or more people.'

'Why are you discussing pronouns?' she asked.

'I'm not.'

'Yes you are.'

'I suppose that this is not really the place,' he said with a wave of his hand.

'No, please continue. I'm enjoying this.' She moved closer to him. 'Seriously, no one else is listening. Just me.'

'Are you happy being by yourself?'

'Is that what it's about? Being happy?'

'Partly.'

'That's disappointing.'

'It's about us. '

'We've been there.'

'I'm not happy without you.'

'Sorry, I didn't catch that. Could you repeat it please?'

'Lara, don't be so difficult.'

'Now it's me being difficult, is it?'

'In fact you're not difficult, you're impossible.'

'Why don't you make your admission?' She nodded at the people on the next table. 'We're all waiting.'

He lowered his voice. 'The admission,' he began.

But she wasn't going to make it easy for him. 'What is it with you and me, Jamie? Why do spend so much time together in cafes? Sorry, I interrupted you.'

'That I need you, Larissa. Without you, I can only get by, and after knowing you, getting by is not enough. Do you believe me?'

'Carry on.'

Speaking so quietly she could hardly hear him, 'I tried to get over you. I met lots of people,' he said, meaning women but she was kind of pleased that he'd said *people*. 'I tried hard not to be with you, to accept the separation, to understand it all. But you were everywhere. Everyone I met reminded me of you by not being you. So I wasn't interested, however perfect they were in other ways. All I knew was that they were not you.'

She wondered what others in the café would think if she cried. Almost certainly that he was giving her some terrible news. She remembered what one of North London's Wise Men had said earlier in the year and took a deep breath. 'I think,' she said, managing to admire her own coolness as she spoke, 'that we'll have a bit less about the perfection of others, if you don't mind,' she said, finding herself giggling, without knowing why. 'And I like the idea of being valued. But I'd quite like to be better than the others as well. Do you think you can manage that?'

'Yes.' And he gave her a particular smile which she felt she hadn't seen for years. *Dear God*, she thought. The idea that she would not have to plan to see him, that he would be there, that the three of them would be back together.

***

And they talked and talked and talked. He told her about life without her and Poppy, and she told him about life without him. They also talked about what had gone wrong without making any great progress on that front. But they spoke enough for her to see how they would speak about it in the future. He would explain and she would believe while at some level she would be doubting what he was saying. But that was ok, she thought. How reliable was her judgment? In any case, you can only doubt so much and then life takes over. You move on.

'Shall we go and get Poppy?' he asked.

She nodded, not really trusting herself to speak. 'I'll order a taxi.'

He stood up. 'Why don't we walk? It's so warm. You know that the snow's almost melted?'

'Yes I know but we can't walk. It's miles. There's the taxi telephone over there.'

'No, let's walk.'

'Let's get a taxi.'

'Let's walk.'

'For God's sake.'

As they waited in the taxi queue, he said that he had left her Christmas present at his flat.

'Not just your present,' she said.

'I'll bring everything home tomorrow.'

Home. 'Has Poppy phoned you this morning?'

'No, not yet, Larusha. I'll call her in a minute.'

'Your Christmas present isn't ready.'

'How exciting. Are you making it? Have you taken up knitting?'

She laughed. 'No, it's a story, a Christmas story.'

He looked up and down the queue of mostly elderly people. 'I think that we're going to be here a long time. Tell me about it.'

'It's supposed to be a surprise.'

'Then you can at least tell me how it starts.'

'Alright. Well, it starts with two lawyers who know each other very well meeting at court where they are on opposite sides…'

THE END

Acknowledgements

This book is dedicated to Freya Bernard and Kathryn Drew. It would not have been completed without their love and encouragement.

I should also like to thank Susie Hicks, Chiara Gorodesky, Jo Olivier, Louise Deacon, Jane de Beneducci, Julia King, Robert Sharp, Brian O'Gorman, Pete Suart, Alan McIntosh, Barbara Zeitler, Bis Culley, and Shabir Hussain.

Printed in Dunstable, United Kingdom

66563039R00099